This Road is a Detour

A VICTORIA WARD CRIME SERIES

L.A. WARD

Fulton Books
Meadville, PA

Published by Fulton Books 2024

ISBN 979-8-88982-867-9 (paperback)
ISBN 979-8-88982-868-6 (digital)

Printed in the United States of America

He thinks the deed is done and he is free at last. He has her medicine hidden from the caregivers. After all, the medicine will be worth a lot of money on the streets, and that is his ticket out of this place. The dreaded phone call. The police will arrive once he makes the phone call. He will have to make sure everything is in order before he makes the call. He needs those meds because selling them will give him plenty of money for his trip down south. Once down south, nobody will ever question him again about his mom and what happened to her, especially the new manager. She seems to know everything, and she just arrived. *My choices are to leave or kill her as well. I really don't have time to sit and think about killing her. It is much easier to walk off this property and never look back.*

Now he must clean up and get ready for the family members, caregivers, and of course, the police. He gathers all the pizza boxes from the night and day before. Once the food is cleaned up, he runs the sweeper and dusts the furniture. It has been twelve hours since his mother died, but he has so many things to do, and he is tired. He takes a much-needed nap before he begins his cleaning-up process. He has to have his wits about him when the onslaught of people starts.

The phone call. He finally calls the family to let them know Mom is dead! Thankfully, she is gone, and now he can get on with his life. This month has been a long time coming. He agreed to take care of mom in exchange for a place to live and food to eat.

*****

Everything was fine until that manager showed up. We had a nice little drug ring going, where we all could make some extra money and have some fun too. She had to start the cleanup, as she called it. Well, she thought she was doing something great. However, many of the people in my circle just want her dead. She better watch her back—that is all I have to say. The word out on the street is she won't be here in a year. Well, neither will I, so who cares? Mom is dead, I'm in over my head, so it is time for me to press ahead with my plans. There you go. I'm a poet and don't know it.

Putting on my game face, I must be the grieving son. It is imperative that I look upset since I did not make the dreaded phone call until twelve hours after dear old Mom left us. The caregivers want the drugs that they must account for, the police just want this over, and my family is insane. I'm so out of here!

Victoria

Evil has no age limit, no gender, and no remorse. That is where I come in. My name is Victoria. I am in the FBI witness protection program. This is a different kind of program because I still work for the FBI. I now work undercover wherever I am sent.

I decided to finish my education in criminal justice at the University of Central Oklahoma. They have the newest and best criminal justice department in the nation.

The criminal justice program at UCO was established in 1974. However, in the fall of 2010, a separate School of Criminal Justice was created. The course is difficult, but I feel I'm up to the challenge. The requirements for this school can't be as hard as working for the US Customs and Border Protection.

On any given day, the border patrol will arrest more than 1,100 criminals. The main goal, however, is to prevent illegals from coming into the United States. These illegals bring drugs and other contraband, which needs to be stopped.

While working with the border patrol, I worked my way into the most malicious gang in the area. I was able to bring this gang to a stop. They were arrested, put in jail, and sentenced to a lifetime in prison. This all came with a price. The price I paid was giving up my name, my location, and any ties to my lifestyle that I became used to while working with the border patrol. I also had to give up Cindy's Place, which is where young women who have been trafficked by the gangs can get out and get help. I miss Cindy's Place. However, it is better that they do not know where I have gone.

I also learned not long ago that the parents that raised me are not my real parents. They abducted me from my home in Harrah, Oklahoma. When I went into the witness protection program, I requested they keep me in the state of Oklahoma as long as it is safe to do so. I want to continue to look for my real parents.

My first assignment landed me in OKC, where I became vastly aware of human trafficking. Once I was finished, I stayed in Harrah for a few months looking for my real parents. I'm sure if I had been more vocal about my intent, I would have more answers by now. In order to stay alive, I cannot bring attention to myself. Once I was rested, I was given another assignment in Maud, Oklahoma. This is where I was almost killed by a killer gang that feeds and grows off hate. Because of my background, I was sent to learn the gang and disassemble it. This gang is one of the toughest kinds of gangs to defeat as they have nothing left to lose.

My expertise includes assessing a witness or a felon, and sometimes they are the same. I can also blend in and find information that leads to the capture of a current criminal. Since I can relate to all aspects of people and I can do the required paperwork, I am sent to housing projects where the FBI thinks there is fraud and other crimes going on. Sometimes it is easy to spot the evil and destroy it. Other times, it takes me a moment to figure out who is the good guy and who is the evil one.

During my time at this apartment complex, I saw many crimes that were not addressed as the local police were afraid of this gang and what they would do to them. I was not afraid. I was appalled at what I saw. This is my story to the best of my knowledge.

The Gang of Eight, How We Hate

The leader is never seen and issues his commands from his phone, either by text or by calling one of his followers. We are only guessing who the leader is since we don't see him or her and the followers are like little robots doing his bidding.

Tonight is no exception. We have a late party for several of the residents, and he tries to kill the party before it gets started. Okay, that may be a bad choice of words. However, in this case, it is the truth. He calls the police to have them come over because there is too much fun—I mean, noise—and he is upset. I'm getting ready to roll my eyes. This person is irritating me, and I have no clue who he is. He will only come out at night. This is common for evil. In some way, he sounds like a vampire.

The partiers go on having fun, and the gang members leave. We have a blast. This is my getting-to-know-you party. Some of the police stay and have supper with us. They are laughing and telling jokes. I love to see people happy and loving life. One day I will meet this leader of the gang of eight that loves to hate. When the day comes for us to meet face-to-face, the party will be over for this gang. As our party continues, several of the residents begin to become frightful. I ask them what is going on, and they say they are afraid that the office will be targeted because we are all having too much fun. I assure them that will not be the case.

As I wake the next day, I feel that last night is a huge success. The haters are angry, and the good people have had fun. Seems about right. Now we sit back and wait to see if there is any movement. It is usually about this time the haters will try to kill somebody. One of these days this will backfire, and they will be the hunted and then killed. This is just the way life works. You can only suppress a people for so long. Well, the haters can just stew for the weekend. I feel like I have made a huge breakthrough, but I should know that it can't be so easy, at least not for the residents, as they must stay there while I leave and go home.

Never Show Fear

It is Monday. Time to hit my local coffee shop and load up on caffeine as I'm sure I am going to need it. Mondays are usually the craziest.

As I make my way to my office at the Pleasant Valley HillTop Apartments, I am greeted by several of what I assume are the members of the gang of eight that hate. I smile and keep my nose in the air. I can't see as well with my nose way up here, but I will not let them see me flinch. Never let fear show. Once these gangs think you are fearful, then it is over. Thank God I have gone through so much gang training. However, I think that the training and the experience I have had taking down drug lords will not help me with this evil gang machine. I will begin training on housing-complex gangs as soon as I get my office in working order.

I open the door and see several rooms that are a mess. I walk to what is my office. The desk is stacked full of papers that make no sense to me at this time. It's dusty and dirty with very little organization. My desk has mounds of paperwork, just what I wanted to see. When I move some of the papers, I see that the top drawer of the desk does not work and there are cigarette burns all over the desk. How will I ever be able to work in this environment? First thing, all papers go to the file room, and then we pull out one box at a time to get them organized. Next the furniture must be replaced.

The floor is very old tile. Some of the rooms had a dirty yellow carpet in it. The paint on the walls is peeling. The color appears to be puke yellow. This color is enough to make anybody sick. Once through the room that appears to be my office, I move to the file room, my bathroom, and an extra closet. These other rooms must be worse than my office if that is even possible. I see boxes and boxes of papers that have been wet, from what, I don't know, and full of mouse droppings. Well now, how long will it take me to clean this place so I can begin work? My new assistant is going to have to be able to clean as well as do paperwork.

The front bell begins to ring. Wow! Something actually works in this place. I go to answer the bell, and it is a young woman whose name I soon learn is Jill Jones. Interestingly, wonder if anybody ever calls her JJ? As she begins to talk, that soon turns into a whine. I really need to have time to sleep, and I need to be exempt from the inspections. By now I'm quite confused. I tell her, "Okay, I will check into that and get back with you." She continues to whine as she walks away on her walker looking all bent over. She looks like she is one hundred years old when I think she is only forty. What a sad sight.

I look around, not sure where to start. I decide to go back to my office and begin the cleanup. After I sit at the broken desk that has cigarette burns all over it, I'm trying to decide what will be first in the cleanup. I finally decide I will take all this paperwork to the file room, where I will have to go through it piece by piece until I can get this place back on track and operating smoothly. I always get the assignments with the most paperwork. I take a long breath. Then I smile to myself before I begin to clean up.

When does it end? Just about the time you think you can sit back and enjoy a normal job, life, and thought, somebody calls out of the blue and pulls you back into reality. Only, my reality deals with death and the spirit world, where most of my fighting takes place. Now before you begin to judge me as a bizarre human, turn on the nightly news, and you will see I'm not so crazy.

I continue to clean the office, and I realize it is going to need a redo if I am going to work here and still breathe. It has a dirty yellow carpet that smells bad. And I cannot work with a desk that has cigarette-burn marks all over the top of it. Nice, who thought that burn marks all over the top of the desk would spruce up the desk, or were they so high they just missed the ashtray? Anyway, I will need to buy a new desk once I get the rest of the office cleaned up.

I decide to hire a company that can come in and put new floors down, paint, remodel my bathroom and kitchen in my office, as well as cover the windows in film. While this is taking place, I decide to visit Fox one last time before I head off to Hillbilly Hell.

Fox was the head of a human trafficking ring that operated out of the Oklahoma City apartment complex I was assigned to. It was my first assignment after being placed into protective custody.

Fox used the two girls in the office to meet other girls and bring them to the complex. These two girls also took care of the books and spied on me. They, however, did not have super great minds. Therefore, they just followed orders and received a good pay for doing so. When I was sent to the apartment complex, we thought that there was a lot of activity, and of course we believed drugs was involved. You always believe the obvious first. After being at the complex for a while and doing my research, I realized that human trafficking is so common these days. This should have been obvious to us, but it was not at the time.

It took me several weeks to put the operation together in my mind as well as be able to tell the police.

During my stay at this Oklahoma City apartment complex, we had many murders, which were mostly domestic- or gang-related. This took me off guard, and it was hard to figure out if the murders had anything to do with the missing girls.

This human trafficking operation took a turn for the worse when two girls from my church were taken. These girls were cute, sweet, and trusting. They had good home lives, but they made a friend at the mall, and they wanted to show this friend God. The friend, of course, did not have good intentions and was able to pull the girls in. Once they agreed to go in a car with this person, that was the end of it.

Fox oversaw this human trafficking ring. He and the two girls in the office, who did nothing but snicker the entire time I worked with them, kept the operation running like clockwork. I guess I should have suspected something when the file clerk did not file and the assistant did not assist. Fox was also my boss, and it was hard to get a straight answer out of him. The Bible talks about double-minded men. Fox was one of them. When he talked, I really did want to spit him out of my mind.

The only thing they did not count on in this little operation was me. They tried to get me fired, and they tried to kill me. Okay, getting me fired was one thing, but trying to kill me, that was a big mistake. I was so mad that I could see fire. I buckled down and started following them. Once I figured out what was happening, I went to look for the two girls that were missing from our church, and the rest is history.

Not quite! Fox mentioned that some of the girls came from up north in Pennsylvania. I had to find out if these were the people who abducted me all those years ago.

Visit into Fox's
New Reality

He comes out into the visitors' room, and of course he begins to snicker. Some things will never change.

"Why are you here?" he asks.

I try to explain to him without him guessing what I'm up to. "Remember the last visit we had, you alluded to the fact that some of the girls come from up north in Pennsylvania?" I ask. He just nods his head. "Well, I would like to know more about the operation in Pennsylvania."

So he begins, "The operation is run by two old people, Jack and Lucy. I'm not sure where the operation is, so that could be tricky finding the place."

In my head, I'm thinking, *Oh, I know exactly where this operation is!*

He continues his story, "Jack and Lucy, and now the kids, just keep the girls over a night or two, and then they send them our way. We prep the girls and get them ready for sale."

My blood is boiling now, and I want to shoot him. I keep my cool. "Is that it?"

"Yep," he snickers, "that is all I know."

I wish I did not know that much. I decide to fly to Hillbilly Hell, then I can rent a car for the few days I will be gone. Busting this ring will not take long. However, I have some questions for old Jack and Lucy.

I figure while I'm on the plane, I will read and study the gang information. I will need to bust the gang of eight that loves to hate.

Touchdown

The plane finally touches down. I fly to Pittsburg and take a rental car to the small town where I grew up. I have butterflies in my stomach. I vowed to never come back here. I have got to find out what is going on and stop any more girls from ending up in human trafficking.

I get into my rental car and say a prayer. If God does not protect me from these people, I can still end up on that van. I drive to the old folks' home to visit Jack and Lucy to see if they will confess. It is difficult to know what to say without making them defensive, and then I would not be able to get any information out of them.

As I walk into their room, my legs begin to shake. I feel like a weak little child again. I smile and decide to start with small talk. "How have you both been?" I ask. They look shocked that I would even talk with them. I try to explain my reason for the visit.

"I'm here only because in my new career I discovered the horrors of human trafficking. After the arrest were made and the leader of this ring was in jail, I went to talk with him. He told me that some of his property came from here in Pennsylvania. The organization was run by a couple, Jack and Lucy. I remember growing up, there were several young girls who mainly passed through our home. Were these the young girls he was talking about? And why did you keep me? I was not your blood child. You could have gotten me out of the picture, and nobody would have known."

Jack and Lucy stare at each other in disbelief. I'm sure they never thought I would find out about the family business. As I talk, they stare. Here we go again! Just like Zoe and Maranda snicker all day, these two just stare.

Finally, I look them in the face and demand answers. "Why did you keep me?"

They both look at me with regret and tears. "We loved you, that is why."

By now I ready to blow. However, I try to keep my cool, knowing that is the only way I will get the answers I am looking for.

"You did not love me or you would have left me with my real mom." By this time, I am looking angry and desperate. There is nothing worse than a person who has nothing left to lose. I give it one last shot with a more authoritative voice. "Why did you keep me and not put me on one of those white vans?" I demand.

That is when Jack shot me a look that says "I would kill you now if I could get out of this bed."

"We kept you because we were afraid somebody was looking for you and might notice you since all the white vans were going through Oklahoma before they went to the border. We always wanted to sell your sorry soul but knew that could be the end of our business, so we just let you live. Now I can see that was the wrong choice," Lucy states.

Well, okay, that was harsh and hard to hear, but now I know the truth, and the Bible does say the truth will set you free.

As I shake off my new reality, I ask them if the kids are still running the business. They hesitate, and that is all the answer I need. Now to shut this thing down for good. They know what I am thinking, and this does not sit well with them. "If you are thinking about calling the kids to warn them, think again. I will let your involvement out of the situation right now if you do not warn the kids. But if you warn them, I will see to it that your last days on earth are in a cell, not an old folks' home. Do you understand me?" They just look at each other and don't say much. So I get in Jack's face, knowing he calls the shots. "Do you understand me?"

He just shakes his head. "We understand. God forgive us for letting our children down."

I roll my eyes. Oh, brother, all they care about is letting their children down. How about the children that they stole and sold? Oh, that's right, they belong to somebody else, so no worries. Yes, I'm sure God will forgive you for letting your kids down.

"Whatever!" I screamed.

Sometimes you have to scream even if it will do no good. People like this, that have no idea what right and wrong is, will never get it. And what will they tell God about abducting me and others? We lost our families, and our families suffered.

Back to My Old Home

This road may have brought me home, where I grew up, but it will never be my home again. When I get this ring shut down, I never want to see this place again. This road may be a dead end, but it does need to be closed. I must finish what I started in Oklahoma City. In my wildest thoughts, I would never have thought the people that I lived with most of my life are the people that started and ran this human trafficking ring. Once this is done, I can go back to Oklahoma and never look back. Going forward will be easier.

My first stop should be the FBI unit that is in this town. They are the only people that I would trust at this point. They can decide who else to let in on this crime. Once at the FBI office, I explain who I am and what I have found out. Then I explain that we must stop the kids as they are more ruthless than Jack and Lucy are, or at least that is how I remember it. I'm sure the kids just want to double any profits Jack and Lucy made. After all, isn't that what you do when you are handed a family business, you grow it and make even more money so that your parents will be proud of you?

When I enter the FBI headquarters at 3311 East Carson Street Pittsburgh, Pennsylvania 15203, (412) 432-4000, I want to talk to them directly so they can get me in touch with the office in Altoona. I am sent to talk with Special Agent Scott Ward.

Scott listens to my story I explain about my one last visit to Fox. I explained that I just could not help myself, I needed to know why. Why do they hide in plain sight and prey on the weak and innocent?

I go on to tell Scott about Fox's explanation and my reaction.

"With a snicker, Fox began to tell me that money was his main motivation. Once he was into the trafficking, he realized he liked the money and it was hard to back out. Zoe was sent to the property to keep an eye on me as she is really the head of this organization. I just nod so he kept talking to me. Of course, he snickered, 'You think that by stopping one ring of human traffickers, you saved the world, but you did not.' Fox went on to explain that before our girls were sent out of the country, they came from a place somewhere in Pennsylvania. As Fox talks, I began to feel sick. He keeps talking about the place up north that is run by a mom-and-pop type. As he tries to remember the details, he comes up with two names, Jack and Lucy! That is all I heard as he was starting to fade from my reality. I'm staring at him like I just saw a spirit and it was evil. I managed a smile and walked away. I will shut that place down!"

After listening to my entire story, Scott then calls some of the other agents in so we can devise a plan to shut this thing down once and for all.

I explain my situation, how I was kidnapped as a baby by these two people and that I ended up in this family until I was married. Once they ended up in the home for old people, they had a sliver of conscience and wanted to tell me the truth. After I learned the truth, I realized I did not have to stay in this family anymore, and I did not have to stay married to a man that acted just like my adoptive (or is that abductive?) father. I divorced and went to Oklahoma to search for my parents. I never thought I would come back, and I never gave this place a second thought. But here I am, and now I want this operation shut down for good.

Jack and Lucy did tell me they would not interfere with the operation because I told them I would have to lump them in with this bust and they would spend time in jail, not in the cozy room they are in now.

As the unit decides how to best proceed, I try to relax. Yeah, right! Let's get this over with so I can get back to my new life. My new life has a few pieces of reality that tend to lean toward the bizarre, but in my new reality that I made with God, it will never be as crazy as the one that was made up for me by these two sickos.

The plan is for me to go to my house and surprise the kids with a visit. While talking with them, I will try to find out as much as possible without letting them know that I'm on to them. I will be wired, and if I cannot find any paperwork or information, I will let the team know I am leaving. If this happens, we will watch the house until we find the girls coming and going. After all, they will not want to stop the flow of money for long.

As I drive up to the house, my stomach begins to get sick. Funny, I never felt this way when I lived here, but I never did fit in either. I breathe and get out of my car. I ring the doorbell, and the kids answer the door. I see a little girl inside playing and laughing. This must be Jack and Lucy's grandchild. The kids are shocked to see me. I smile and state I've come home for a visit. They introduce me to Julie, their little girl, and I ask her some questions. They send her to her room for the rest of the visit.

I smile and take a seat in the living room. "How have you been?" I ask. They both start talking at one time like they really did miss me, or they were very nervous. They offer me some coffee, and I decline. I remember some of those young girls always look like they are on drugs of some kind. I am not going to take any chances. They do not seem to care one way or another. They want to know about me and my new life. That is easy to talk about. What? I have parts that are real and not made up. I begin to tell them about Meme, and they think that is amusing. Why do I not see any young girls around? Well, here goes. Let's get it out.

"After Jack and Lucy went to the home, did you all keep up with foster kids, or did you stop that?"

They looked amused. They start to snicker, and I just roll my eyes. What the heck, is snickering a part of this business?

"We still do foster caring. We have scaled back a little. We take only children that need a place to stay for a couple of nights, then they move on."

And in my mind, I can't help myself. I want to say, "Do they leave in a white van?" I just smile and talk about the decorations in the house.

Julie, Jack and Lucy's grandchild, comes running out of her room and wants to know if I am staying for supper, and are her friends coming to play with her tonight? I think the kids are going to drop dead right then and there. That will have solved a lot of problems and saved time. *Stop it!* I chide myself. *God is in control, not you.*

They assure Julie that Aunt Victoria has other places to go and that her friends can come play tonight. Bingo! Just what we need to know. Tonight is the night we stop this ring of human traffickers.

The Ring Is Broken

I GO BACK TO FBI headquarters and tell them everything. I remind them that if they want to bust up this human trafficking ring, they should move tonight. I explain that Julie, who is my niece, have asked if her friends are coming to play after supper tonight. I know what she is talking about as I remember many young girls coming through our home and only staying a night or two then are gone. When I asked where they went, my mother, Lucy, would always tell me they were foster kids and that they only stayed a couple of nights until they were place in permanent foster homes. I thought that made complete sense and would love having them come and play with us for a while. We had wonderful suppers and playtime. Then the white van would come and pick them up, and we would never see them again. I was always so happy for them because I thought they were on their way to a more permanent home. It made me feel proud that our family was helping them along the way. Now I want to puke when I think of what Jack and Lucy did to these young girls. I guess that is how they can afford the nursing home in their final days.

The FBI unit agrees we move tonight and stop this ring of human traffickers. How does a person sell another human? I just hate it, but I am happy "the kids" are going to get what is coming to them.

In 2014, the FBI's Civil Rights Unit along with special agents throughout the country participated in more than 100 human trafficking task forces. They identified 600 victims and 400 separate cases. The FBI opened more than 500 child sex trafficking investigations and convicted more than 350 subjects for their roles in the commercial sexual exploitation of children (*Human Trafficking Ring Dismantled*, 01/27/2015). The FBI has no problem shutting down these human trafficking rings, and I have no problem helping them.

They decide to send a car to watch the house. They will watch the house until it is time to act. Once it is time to act, it will not take much time to round up everybody, and the kids won't know what hit them. I wish I could see their faces, but I will be on a plane on my way back to my current assignment. The director of the FBI unit promises to let me know when it is all over. I thank him and go on my way knowing that this sick family is not going to hurt any other families ever again.

Flying Back to My Current Reality or My Current Assignment

As I sit on the plane, I look at the information that I found about adult bullying. Breaking up this bullying group will not be easy; I need to read up on them or at least the kind of group they represent so that I can be better prepared. If there is one thing I've learned in my short career, it's that you should always look like you know what you are talking about.

The APA, or the American Psychological Association, defines *bullying* as "a form of aggressive behavior in which someone intentionally and repeatedly causes another person injury or discomfort" (*5 Ways that Adults Bully Each Other*).

In the case of the elderly or adults bullying at this complex, I am told it is mostly verbal to begin with. This is not uncommon. Verbal bullying will consist of threats, shaming, hostile teasing, insults, and constant negative judgment (*5 Ways that Adults Bully Each Other*).

The other type of bullying that is usual among elderly and adults is passive-aggressive or convert bullying. This is not quite as easy to spot. It usually shows up in the form of negative gossip, negative joking at someone's expense, sarcasm, and deliberately causing embarrassment and insecurity. This form of bullying will cause isolation and take away from the joy and happiness of the victim (*5 Ways that Adults Bully Each Other*).

An ancient Chinese proverb states, "Behind the smile is a hidden knife." Guess at one time there was a Chinese person who lived at this complex.

While this proverb describes bullying, it also described living in Hillbilly Hell for all those years.

I always ask, "Why, why do people become bullies?" In the case of the housing complex, most older adults that become bullies do so out of boredom (how stuff works). In my training for my job, it was suggested that if I would find something for them to do, they would stop being bullies. I'm sure the shock on my face was evident. These were grown adults, and rather than holding them accountable for their actions, I was told to babysit them and find something for them to do. I just nodded my head when that was suggested. Now I'm reading about these evil monsters to find a way to remove them, not coddle them. Our society has gotten so far off the path of right that it makes me want to scream. But I know if I disagree, I will never find out who is the head of this monster group, and I will never be able to find out what their weakness is so I can beat them at their own game.

As I continue to read the information given to me by my FBI contact, I am still shaking my head. The gang of eight that loves to hate is bored, and I should find them a hobby. I'm assuming a hobby that does not include killing and torturing the other residents. Poor little gang members, they are just so misunderstood. Yeah, right! I will show them misunderstood. One way to throw idiots off track is to stick to the rules and smile. By smiling, they never can figure out what your next move is.

Including being a gang, there is usually a mob mentality that shows up. They believe that if they are in a gang or a mob, nobody can hurt them. Hurt them—does anybody ever think about all the people who suffer at the hands of gangs? It makes my skin crawl when I think of how people gang up on the weaker group around them. It is always the weaker ones that end up getting hurt in all this. In the case of this apartment complex, I am told there have been several unexplained murders, several people who have become missing and never heard from them again. The administration seemed to be in on it, whatever it is.

I should get some sleep before the plane lands, and I must begin my next fight. Some get adventures. I get battles.

My New Reality

The next day I get up and get ready for work. I'm so tired mentally after dealing with Lucy and Jack and the kids I just want to sleep for about a week. No such luck. I must get into the office so that I can see what kind of mess I need to begin cleaning up. I take a shower, hoping this will help me wake up. It does wake me up, but I am going to need some serious caffeine today. Lucky for me, I don't live too far from a fantastic coffee house. It is drive-through as well, so I can get my caffeine on the run today. I think I will order a pound of chocolate-covered espresso beans as well. That might sound over the top, but unless you have tried them, and tried them from my favorite coffee house, you can't judge me. You have no idea what you are missing. At this rate, I will be quite alert all day. Yes! My kind of day: caffeine-induced! I had a doctor once ask me if I drank caffeine. I just laughed and stated, "I would take it intravenously if I could."

Once I have my coffee, espresso beans, and yogurt from my favorite coffee house, for healthy eating, I head to the office. As I pull into the property, the first thing I see is the grass needs cut, the weeds need to be pulled or just killed off, and flowers need to be watered. Who has been taking care of this place? Wait, I can answer that, nobody! By now I'm really upset that this place looks so dark and so sad. Now it is time for an infusion of God's light into this place. We are going to see things grow and see things look happy again. I will find the evil and remove it from this property.

The Office

I THOUGHT THAT I cleaned up some of the fraud and evil on the property before I left for Pennsylvania. How was I supposed to know that evil will stay around in many other forms? I really did not spend a lot of time here before I had to leave to tie up all the loose ends from my last assignment. I just never thought it would include my family and Hillbilly Hell. Now that I fought that fight and put the evil in jail, this would be my next challenge.

I try and try to remove the evil, but it keeps coming back. Now I must separate the good from the wicked. I will start with the vile assistant that I hired in a hurry to keep the office open while I was gone. That was a big mistake. I'm sure I will make many mistakes before this assignment is over. I just wish I did not have to get a new assistant so soon. This person is a piece of work. She is having sex with all the men, she is plotting behind my back with all the drug dealers, and she is working with the gang of eight. She could have had a great career here, but not now. She must go. I walk into the office a little early, and she is shocked to see me back early. What is that look for? Have I interrupted something? I just bet she knows who is running this gang. Heck, she is probably in charge of the gang since I left her alone for a few days.

We exchange nice words of greeting, and she tells me enough to keep me off her back for now. I notice that my checks are a mess, which I keep in my desk, and that some are missing. Lola always seems to be where she is not allowed to be. I must get a camera installed in this office. I know Lola is doing more things behind my back, but up until now she has been sly and I have been busy.

Not now! Game on! She thinks she can get away with anything. I'm smarter and cuter. I also love God and fight for him. We will see who is the strongest, my God or her god.

In the days to come, all hell was breaking loose, not only on the property, but also in my office. I can't wait until it is time to get this person out of my office.

The Assistant from Hell

I KNOW THAT NOW you are thinking about every slasher movie you've ever seen. Well, she is not that kind of hellish assistant. She actually starts out nice and helpful. I was hoping we could form a bond of some kind and work together on this assignment. We clean the file room together, and as we do, she confesses to be a Christian, which is good. I take her at her word. Now, that is where I make my mistake. Do not take people at their word. Duly noted! That is a hard lesson to learn. What is that Air Force motto? "In God we trust. All others we monitor." Works for the Air Force. I think I better remember that.

I have so many irons in the fire that I really do need help, and I let my guard down. Once I get some things under control, I start noticing weird things, like I always have checks missing. Checks that have to be mailed to the accountant. No matter what system I come up with, I always lose checks. I misplace other important paperwork as well. Of course, this makes me look suspicious to the accountant from hell. The accountant tells me in no uncertain terms that he was in charge. He pats my head and tells me to shut up and color. I can assure you I am seeing red about now. I have practiced keeping my emotions in check. Okay, I roll my eyes and state that I am the one in charge, and that if anything goes down on this property, I will be the blame. But then the accountant knows that. Now we both know where we stand.

I am starting to think that I'm going crazy. She is a good mind player.

She has one weakness that will be her downfall: she loves men and food. Okay, that will be two weaknesses. We have several maintenance men that will do her bidding at any time. Little by little, I am weeding out the ones that are not at the complex to just work. We had a huge emergency one day, and I realize then I need to hire a maintenance person that is going to be my ally. We are in the middle of chaos, and her sidekick, maintenance man number 1, Brandon, states that he knows where we can find some help. He gives me the name of a temp agency, and I begin to hire temps for a while.

One day I am talking to the man in charge of the temp agency, and he states he has a maintenance person that just may work out for us. I confirm that this new temp will know maintenance work and be able to fix things as well as work under pressure. I am assured he will be perfect.

The Interview

I HAVE LOLA AND Brandon sit in on the interview as a kindness as they are a part of this team that I am trying to build. In walks Michael! Michael is tall and thin. He seems to be rather quiet, and I'm not sure he will fit in at first. Lola, of course, is eyeing up his body, and Brandon wants to make sure that Michael is not going to outdo him. After the interview is over, I walk Michael to the door while Lola and Brandon have time to talk, behind my back, of course.

When I go back into the room, I ask them what they think. Both are very positive about the fact that Michael is all wrong for the job. I listen to both of their arguments, and I ask a few questions. Once we are done consulting with one another, I announce that I am going into call the temp agency and I am going to hire Michael for the full-time job in maintenance. Stunned by this statement, they just get up and leave.

After my decision to hire Michael, the games begin. Michael is fast and appears to be smart. What is that old saying? Don't judge a book by the cover? Mistake number 2. I start to trust Michael, and he would continue to play me. Little do I know that Michael is hoping he will someday run the show himself. For now, it is me and Michael, which appears to work. Things are not always as they appear. Does this trust issue ever end?

Trust

I DON'T KNOW WHOM to trust. Now I must continue with my plans of replacing my evil assistant. I thought I could trust my staff, but I find out that they are in on all the evil that is happening around here.

As it turns out, the only thing I have managed so far is to clear my office of all the deception and immoral activity. Evil is still lurking in the front office and the rest of the building, as well as outside on the grounds. This is going to be a long battle, I can tell.

When I finally realize that all roads don't lead home, I'm wondering where home is. My best friend and longtime roommate, Anna is always looking for her next adventure, and I always end up with the next battle. Today is no different. I get myself together. I must find a human I can trust so that we can pray over this property and make it great again like the founders wanted it to be. So much evil, so little time. Okay, that is kind of funny. I must take the funny any place I can get it at this point.

Michael

Michael, can I trust him? He seems to be quiet and a good worker. I will try to build a working relationship with him. Today I will have him work in the office, where there is a lot of woodworking and other things that need to be done. Let's see if he is somewhat trustworthy.

While Michael appears to be smart and trustworthy, it is because he knows how to play mind games even better than my mentor, my ex-husband. He will keep me informed, but he uses lies. Truth seems to be out of his range. He lies even when he does not have to. He works his way into the females' apartments and has sex with them as he confuses them. I'm getting ahead of myself as I never knew this in the beginning since he kept me confused as well.

Michael is working out well. However, Lola is breathing down his neck all the time. I finally talk to Michael, and he states that Lola wants him to come work for her at her house. She also offers "other things" as well. I suggest that he uses the side door to my office and not go through Lola's office. He agrees, and we begin to bond as a team (at least it appears that way). Now I have to push Michael to help me rid my property of Brandon and Lola. He is very agreeable. Brandon will be the first to go.

What is that Chinese saying? "The enemy of my enemy is my friend." I think it came from a book or something about the art of war.

This is war.

The players

- Peter: Michael's friend that is working in the maintenance department
- Apollyon: a name given to Satan and his minions

- Michael: hired to work with Brandon and now works against him
- Lola: evil assistant
- Gang leader: We do not know who this person is
- Victims of the gang that have been threatened or killed by this gang

I find out later that Lola is coming by the complex so she can form alliances with the evil residents that are living at the complex. The reason: to destroy me. She is cunning, and she does not let very many people in on what she is doing. She has her little group that is becoming stronger and larger in numbers.

Finally, the maintenance person and I form a bond, and we help each other with regard to keeping an eye on the office and the building, which means watching Lola.

I must trust somebody at this point, and Michael seems to be the best choice.

I always feel like somebody is going through my office. I start to watch my back even closer. I must take files home with me and lock everything up even tighter than it has been. Ultimately, Lola realizes she is getting nowhere, so she starts to make friends with the residents and find several groups of gang members that will take up with her. This is her final move. The maintenance man and I are watching her. She can't get away with much.

I tell Lola, the assistant from hell, that I need to take tomorrow off so that I can go to the doctor's and get my meds refilled. Of course, she is happy about that so she can have Michael all to herself and she can get the residents upset even more than they are. Nothing I can do because I need to see this stupid doctor, and he must make sure I don't have to come back for another six months so I have time to work on my property.

Brandon is as evil as the assistant, but not quite as smart. Lola and Brandon love to make fun of me as I pass through the front office. I'm the little hillbilly girl that is trying to run the show, and they think they have me beat. We will see who has the most street skills and survives. Brandon talks dirty, and the assistant seems to like it. She likes any man that will pay attention to her. At this point in our little relationship, I can only guess that she had a bad childhood and that is what makes her roll the way she does. Isn't that what we blame everything on? We had a bad childhood, or a mother that did not understand me, or we did not get all the Christmas cookies we wanted. No wonder *Dr. Phil* is still on the air.

I'm sure Lola will have the time of her life running the office. How could I have believed a person from my old property management job when they gave Lola a good reference? As it turns out, they still are hiding something on that property, and this is their way of getting even with me. Bad mistake! I will be back someday when they least expect it.

Michael keeps tabs on Brandon and reports anything that is out of the ordinary. Once we figure out Brandon is stealing from the company, it is goodbye to him. That is easy. Lola, on the other hand, will be a little harder as I am not going to pay any unemployment to her. We watch her like a hawk. We begin to never leave her alone. She then begins coming to the complex after hours. Now what the heck is that all about? Once I discover this, I begin to do a camera check every single morning. I must come in early and get caffeinated sooner, but it is worth it.

We must learn from our mistakes and get better.

Mistake no. 1!

After living with Lola in this office environment for a very short time, I learn a huge lesson about trusting people you really are not close with: you can't! This is a simple but painful lesson to learn. After all my time in gang territory, you would think I should have known this. Now I will have to remove her from the office and sure hope that is soon. I know it sounds like you can just walk in and fire an employee, but it is not that easy. Criminals always make mistakes, and when they do, I can step in and fire them.

Going to the doctor's is never my favorite thing. And the crazy doctors hold your medicine hostage until you show up for tests. How sane is that? My theory is better to be healthy and not need all those meds. As if I can. I try, but I'm not resting or eating right. That will hurt anybody. The stress is starting to mound as well, hence the reason for not eating or sleeping. I see evil in every corner of the property. Maybe I am the one that is beginning to go insane. Growing up in Hillbilly Hell, I did not receive the best food or health care, so I did not get a great start. This is the reason that doctors and dentists are never my favorite place to go. I remember once when I was in first grade, the school called Lucy and told her to take me to the dentist. Jack never believed in the kids, which included me, going to the doctor's or the dentist. Now that I think back on it, what would he know about going to the dentist? He did not have any teeth, except the ones that stayed in a medicine cabinet for those special occasions. Back in the day, or maybe it was just what Lucy wanted to pay for, the dentists were terrible. No pain-killing methods whatsoever. I used to hyperventilate when I had to go to the dentist because of my childhood days. Now I just make sure they have plenty of laughing gas on hand and call it good.

Mistake no. 2!

I usually make mistakes daily, but this is a huge mistake. We need to have doctor's offices that have drive-through windows. This will save time.

Because I took yesterday off to go to the doctors, that one act would be a huge mistake. I guess you could say all hell broke loose. The maintenance man tries to pick and choose who stays in this apartment complex that I'm managing. Then the residents that don't trust him start a war with him. Therefore, the bully group is stirred up, and they are using a mob mentality to break down the good and decent people in this place. I suspect that I have somebody who is poisoning the residents and somebody who is just scaring people, in some cases to death. Okay, people, the killing must stop. Let's get a grip here. That would be a good place to start.

If that wasn't enough, I find out that several of the men had been date-raped over the weekend. Several women drugged the guys and took advantage of them. It sounds crazy, but the men were victims.

Of course, I must prove all this, and that could take time. I don't dare eat any of the food that is offered to me, or I could be the next victim. Now I know that sounds crazy and you are probably wondering how many times a day I get food offered to me, well, the answer would be a lot actually, thanks for asking. At first, I think it is nice that somebody cares. Then I realize, oh, they care all right—they care that I am still here and alive.

Have you ever heard, "Keep your friends close and your enemies closer"? So I take the food, smile, and say, "Thank you." When the assistant isn't looking, I throw it away. I'm sure they are wondering about my insides. How I can eat all that poison and live? That will keep them guessing.

Random Camera Check

I DO RANDOM CAMERA checks when I get to work so I can see what is going on. I decide to take the section of time that I was off property to go to the doctors to see what was happening.

What to my wondering eyes should appear, it is not eight tiny reindeer? There is Lola talking to members of the gang of haters. Why should I be surprised? I can only imagine what she was up to.

They talk for a while, then she comes back into the office. I watch the gang go their separate ways. In the meantime, I find out that June died, and April was the last person to be seen with her. Did she kill her? June was the one in charge for a very long time. She would tell the board things about me that were not true, and she ran this place out of fear. April was a wannabe. She wanted to be June, but she was not as smart or as mentally stable.

Lola takes June's death very hard, which surprises me. April begins to act very sure of herself. Is she June's replacement? Now that is a scary thought. Once I see this, I decide to look at footage from about a week ago. There is June standing in front of her apartment, and here comes Lola after hours to talk with her.

Watching the cameras only make my life that much more unsure. I feel like I'm completely alone with nobody to trust. Then in walks Michael. I sure hope I can trust this guy and that I'm not making a deal with the devil himself. Time will tell.

Michael smiles and asks if I need anything and if he has any work orders. I tell him about the camera watch and what I saw. He seems interested. He never does stay in character very long. I think he is so busy keeping the building together. The leader is the only person that does not seem to care how well we keep the building and how much we give the residents. He, the leader, puts hate out there and watches where it goes.

Back to the cameras, I need the cameras to stay one step ahead of the evil gang in this place.

Assistant Makes Her
Fatal Mistake

Finally she makes a fatal mistake, and one of the residents turns her into me. When I ask her to explain, she just smiles and states, "Why don't you fire me?" I go home that night, pray, write her up, and give her what she wants. I fire her the next day.

It is time to fire the assistant from hell. I did not think this would be easy, but I did not think it would take forever. Lucky for me that Michael is on my side, or at least he pretends to be, and I have a very good attorney. As we prepare for Lola to come in, I ask her to come back to my office. She thinks she is going to be in on some good gossip. I tell her that I want her keys and that I was letting her go. She, of course, is shocked. I'm not sure why she is shocked, but she is. After all, just yesterday, she told me she wanted me to fire her. She takes the keys off her person and hands them to me. After that, we go to her desk, and as she is cleaning out her personal effects, she tries to go through some files. I tell her to get out of them, that they belong to the company. Once again, she looks shocked and bewildered. I can't wait to see what she was hiding in those files.

As the days continue into weeks, we continue to monitor the situation. I try my hardest to hire a new assistant, and that is not going well. Not because it is hard to find somebody to take Lola's place. After all, finding somebody to steal from me, go after the maintenance man sexually, and form pacts behind my back will not be hard. On the other hand, finding somebody I can live with each day in the same office will not be easy.

During this entire time, Michael acts like he is happy to help me and will testify against Lola if needed. He helps me clean out her desk, and we begin to prepare for the next assistant. Michael, as it turns out, is a control freak, and as long as he can control what is happening, he does not go off the rails.

Feeling Alone

Finding the right person for the office is almost as difficult as dealing with the gang of eight. I know that the person sitting at that front desk will have to be strong and take a lot of abuse from these crazy people. It is not easy being in service type of jobs, especially when you have so much evil to contend with.

I sit at my desk and cry because my brain is overworked and I'm so alone. They say what does not kill you makes you stronger. Really? I don't feel super strong right now, and who would they be anyway? This is a battle of wits and a battle of good and evil. The fact that it is Halloween does not help either. Sounds crazy, but these people seem to be even more bizarre now, you know, full moon and all.

Wow, things happen really fast around here. June was the old woman who ran the place for many years. I really never trusted her, but I did put up with her for the time I knew her. I always had my eye on her, and to be honest she did take some of the work off me so that I could get the paperwork under control. After all, I love paperwork! Not! One day I realize that nobody paid the taxes on my property for the past five or six years. I must work with the city to make a deal in order to bring all taxes current.

The tax manager at the city seems fair while I am trying to negotiate with him, and I think all is going well. I am really taken aback when the tax manager and the city manager are sitting in complete darkness while the rest of us are all sitting in the light. Now before I go any further, do we all see a parallel here? Looking at all the players that have showed up and how they are seated, I realize right away this is going to be one of those battles. Once again, I am in the middle of a spiritual war. First line of defense against evil, say nothing, listen, and pray like your life depends on it. I shut my mouth, and I started to listen. What comes out of the tax manager's and city manager's mouths shock me. They are stating that I am saying they have not handled the money correctly and that they need my money. Say what? Where do they get that idea?

I just sit there and listen to these two fools. They say one or two words of truth, and they twist everything else. Then I begin to understand what is happening. The tax manager and the city manager were having June spy on me and my staff. She reported to them daily. The only problem is, she only reported half-truths as we did not let her hear everything that was happening in the office, and she twisted what she did hear. She was definitely the spin queen in the spin zone.

After June is killed, I mean after she died, I am talking to the tax manager, telling her what I have found out, that she was actually feeding other people information about us. She was the one calling all the shots for the evil in this place. I think the tax manager is going to drop over. I know at this time I can't trust anybody. I feel like my mistakes just keep piling up.

Follow the Leader,
the Gang's Leader

I AM SO TIRED of that manager. She tries to save all the little uninformed people that are slow. She makes some progress. I cannot figure out how she can stay one step ahead of us. I will kill her! I will kill her! the leader thinks to himself or herself.

"She has no idea the power I have and how I can control this little gang of mentally defective people. They follow me around like I'm the god of the housing complex. One day we will meet face-to-face, and then we will see who has the power and who has control of this building.

"Killing June was easy. April was a willing participant as she wanted to take June's place and she wanted to rule the building. What a fool, I am the only one that is going to run this building. April will have to leave soon. She is out of control, and I cannot have people around me that cannot control themselves.

"That manager doesn't realize it, but she talks to me almost every day. You would think she would pick up on the not-so-obvious hints I leave behind. Just goes to prove my theory that a degree does not make a smart person. We will see just how smart she is when I start killing off other people who live here. I'm sure that won't go well with the people over her. After all, if the apartments are empty, she will have to leave, right?" The leader continues the rage.

Trust

Victoria's Trust Issues

Trusting anybody is a mistake at this point in time. One of my biggest tasks is to find somebody I can trust in my own office, and since I can't trust anybody, it will be hard to figure this out. After I pay the taxes, of course. Not only do I owe the city, I owe the feds. The IRS is not very forgiving. I end up emptying the bank account as I pay over $100,000 just in taxes. Now I need to find somebody to work in this office with me that I can trust, and I need to get this bank account in the green, not the red.

Not only do I have to find an assistant, I need one that can handle the evil in this place. With June dead, April begins to emerge stronger. She makes a deal with the devil, Michael, one day. He is always lying to everybody, and April is no exception.

Regrouping

I MUST REGROUP AFTER June died. It is a shock and a relief all at the same time. Another tenant decides she wanted to take June's place. April is already a building manager on the weekends. She, however, is in everybody's business. I try to explain to her that if she just does her job, stays to herself, then she will be fine. Does she follow my instructions? No! Nothing stops her from being just plain crazy. She, of course, is in love with Michael.

She is preparing for a trip. She wants new floors and painting for her apartment. We like to do some of these items when the resident is gone on holiday as it is easier. She clears it with me, good move. However, rather than allowing me to coordinate the upgrade to the apartment, she decides she will go to Michael. She is promised the moon by him, and he does not follow through. Michael is great at promising anything you want to hear because he is not going to follow through anyway.

If Michael does not like you, then he will find a way to remove you from the property. Sometimes he does this through intimidation. Other times he will threaten somebody. I do not notice a pattern until later. He tries this with April, and she just becomes crazier, if that is even possible. I really do feel bad for her as she has chosen the dark side, which makes her even more miserable than she is before. Her strength comes from her hate. She does not belong to the gang, and she is not part of what they are doing. I suppose this is a good thing since her hate becomes stronger and stronger every day. She becomes obsessed with Michael and then me. I try to explain to her that if she talks with me and not Michael, then she will not be going through this stress with the upgrade not being done. Unlike Michael, I do not make promises I can't keep. My word is my bond, and well, you know the rest of it. If I say it, I mean it, and I keep it. This does not seem to help at all. She just hates me more. Now that I think about it, I'm sure Michael keeps feeding her hate to the point if she does not leave, she will have self-destructed. Sometimes I think I am a little slow to discern these things.

I just have to find a good assistant that I can trust. If I can find an assistant that will work with me and not against me, then we can get the office in shape and stand against the evil that is ruling this mob.

Another Day Another Adventure, Right?

Today a drug head decides to go off the deep end when he smokes some bad weed. He rips his clothes off and begins to go after the men in the shack outside on the apartment grounds. Where he got the stuff is what I would like to find out. That video is so hard to watch as Lucifer's demonic group is enticing the group of women in the shack to laugh at the kid on the drugs. He is slithering around like a snake, and they are taking videos like it is funny. I want to gag, but that will show weakness, and you must never show weakness of any kind. The guy that set him up is making him stay in the shack so others can watch him.

You just can't make this stuff up. I know that the maintenance man is behind this. I just need to prove it. Since we have two maintenance men, I need to try and trust one of them. The maintenance man and the assistant from hell. Doesn't get much better than that.

Yesterday a resident decided he could not trust anybody and was building bottle bombs in his apartment then to be sure the people that were watching him did not get into his apartment. He took an extension cord, cut one end off, exposed the wires, tied the exposed wires around the metal doorknob, then plugged it in. This is going to be a long assignment, I can feel it.

The Players as I
Know Them Today

Besides the gang, we have groups of evil that prey on the weak.

The main players that are still standing and fighting are the following.

Donna, who seems to be one of the leaders.

Donna has the blackest short hair I have ever seen. She has very white teeth. Why do I notice her teeth unless in the back of my mind I'm afraid she will bite me? How crazy is that? Maybe not so crazy. I won't' give her that chance.

Sarah, who is Donna's shadow. Donna does not seem to like Sarah. However, they seem to stick together like glue. Sarah has silver-blond hair with blue eyes. Her teeth are fang-like, almost like a vampire. To my knowledge, she has never bitten anybody, but who knows? I've only been here a short time. Donna appears to always tell Sarah what to do. Why do adults allow others to bully them? Why do bullies act the way they do? My only guess to the second question is the control. The whole world is full of control freaks.

What is a control freak about anyway? *Psychology Today* explains it this way. People who are control freaks need a high level of control. This anxiety-ridden person believes that the world would not turn in the correct way at the correct time if they do not control as much as they can. When I was married, I used to feel this way. I can remember cleaning was my drug of choice. When I was stressed, I would clean. I was not allowed to work outside the home, so I cleaned, cooked, and cleaned some more. I cleaned because it was the only thing I could control. If my house was clean, then the world was spinning correctly, and my husband would be happy with me. Not that it ever worked, he wasn't happy with me no matter what I did, no matter how clean the place was, and no matter what I cooked or what I wore.

Once I was out of the abusive relationship and found peace of mind, I realized that being a control freak is very exhausting. It is very draining when you must make sure people in your life are doing exactly what you think they should be doing. And the crazy thing is he still ran around on me and still abandoned me.

Now that I am free, I just smile and go on. I smile a lot because I know where my freedom comes from. Now I must face the fact these bullies want to control me. Good luck with that.

Donna, on the other hand, needs and likes the control because it gives her purpose in life. She deems herself the savior in this small world she has created. Now that I am in her space, she is worried her world is going to spin out of control. I now must put the pieces together and see if she is willing to do anything to try to keep control, even murder.

Sarah appears to be weak and Donna's yes-girl. She also looks like she is on some heavy drugs, or off her drugs, not sure which the truth is currently. This is another issue that will have to be taken care of. Usually if they are off the drugs, that can be dangerous not for them but for me as one never knows what they are capable of. And let's throw in a full moon for good measure. That always makes things interesting.

Crow, who I think is the leader, but I'm not sure.

Crow does not show his face often, and when he does, he always has his little followers around. They act like sheep being led to slaughter. Crow never smiles and never has anything good to say. He is from all appearances sad, bitter, and very evil. But I don't think he has ever bitten anybody. What is with me and the biting thing? From all the chatter, he would bite if he could. What about murder? That goes beyond biting.

Jane was friends with June, and now that June is dead, she is one of the silent followers. She lives in her own bubble. Since the departure of our sweet little June, Jane has become more ferocious and aggressive. Jane appears to be selling drugs. She pretends not to hear you, and yet she seems to know everything that is going on. One day she is outside waiting for her usual pickup. I decide that will be the best time to become her best friend. I go outside and talk to her, asking all kinds of questions. She is so nervous it is almost funny. To my surprise, the drug drops end that day at the front of the building. Jane does not want to go to jail. She is too old and wants only to pad her income. I'm sure she will take the deals else were now.

This list is not complete at all as these are just the players I know so far. I would like to believe there is an easier way to make a living. I can't believe the paperwork and the head games this assignment entails. Did I mention I hate paperwork?

Donna and Sarah are the scariest. At least the scariest I've seen to date. When you look into their eyes, there is nothing. It is hollow, like they have no soul. Then they smile at you knowing they are thinking about how they can take you out. I'm pretty sure that they could kill you and then go out for lunch. Okay, it sounds like I'm working in a mental hospital. Not really. There is just a lot of crazy going around. And I'm not trying to be a drama queen. It is just coming out that way.

What to do? What to do? I smile back at them and pretend I don't know anything. I never show fear! Which is rather funny because that is what gangs want: it's for you to fear them. Oh, to be back in the sane world of drugs and gangs at the border. They were predictable. I hate to say this, but at least those gangs were not mental. With all this happening it is time, I need to get an assistant in here that I can trust.

If it isn't bad enough that I can't trust the players, I have a group of overseers that are like a board that are as untrustworthy as the players. I'm sure some of the players are reporting to the overseers. I'm not sure what they are reporting, and I'm sure they are making things up as they go. What to do? What to do? This is just plain exhausting not having anybody to talk with or trust.

> The perfect assistant
> Honest
> Loyal
> God-fearing

Wants to work
Will work with me (team player)
Doesn't need to lust after the maintenance man
Is smart and can think through problems

Okay, this seems like an impossible list, but somebody out there must fit this description.

I continue to try new assistants. One assistant lasted a day. He was quite the gem.

It will not have worked anyway. Seems our Michael does not like competition. This is in his mind only.

Okay, now I'm getting desperate. I can do the job entirely by myself, but not for long. That will mean coming in at 6:00 a.m. each day and working until 5:00 p.m. A schedule like that will burn you out on a job quickly. I have one final call to see if my old friend is ready to go back to work after having several children. On the other hand, having several children, she may need to come back to work for some peace. We will see.

Hiring Daniella

I DECIDE I SHOULD be more aggressive with searching for an assistant. I go through several. I am almost at the end of my rope when I think about Daniella. She worked with me once before, and we seem to work well together. At this point, I have nothing left to lose and everything to gain.

I call Daniella and ask her to come and work with me temporarily until I can find somebody permanent. She agrees!

Daniella is so smart, and she has a handle on what needs to be done to make our office work. Now this does not make Michael happy. Michael begins turn into the darkness even faster than before. Daniella is wise and can see how he is evolving into evil.

We both try to work with Michael, and it is hard to keep up with him and keep up with all the things inside the office that need to get done. He is in the habit of coming and going in the office that we never know when he will show up. We notice that he will try to listen to our conversations and use them against us.

Time passes quickly, and it comes time for Daniella to leave. I still do not have a lead on a good assistant. So I do the only thing a self-respected executive director would do: I beg her to stay. I offer flex hours and a huge raise. She stays, much to my relief.

We work to set up a routine that will work for both of us. She works at the front of the office, and I take care of the administration part. We both begin to plot how to remove the evil.

Daniella and I work on several missions together when we served in the FBI and not in this crazy witness protection program. Daniella had two children by then. I was sent to the witness protection program, and she quit to have more babies. I did, however, keep her phone number through all the missions and separations.

I figure if anybody can help me get this place together, she can. Daniella is a no-nonsense type of person. She shows very little emotion and just sees the facts. Once she came, we began to work on some kind of order. She is almost done with her temporary time frame. This is where I begin to beg. I really need her to stay with me and form a team that we can trust. I thought at first it would be me, Daniella, and Michael as the three musketeers.

Daniella doesn't usually say much to those around her, and she holds her comments unless it is a game changer, then she will talk with me about it. It has been great since Daniella has been here, and now it is time to beg. I ask her to consider staying on with me. She is already certified in many areas that I am. She has the same temperament that I do. What can go wrong?

She thinks about it and says she will stay. I assure her that she can come and go as she pleases, and she can run the front office. Yes, this is the beginning.

We begin to put the office back together and start again. We begin to have fun in the office. This, of course, threatens Michael. He begins to do peculiar things to get my attention as if he is a boyfriend or my son. How crazy is that? Daniella and I just shake our heads. But we begin to realize we need to keep an eye on him. Michael can jump from light to darkness faster than anybody I know. He also lies more than anybody I ever talked to before in my life. Daniella and I have a hard time separating the lies from the truth. After a while, it is making us tired just trying to figure out the lies. We decide to lean toward everything that comes from his mouth is a lie. As I am talking with Daniella, I ask her if she knows what the Bible states about the Father of Lies. She states, "No, I do not."

> You belong to your father, the devil, and you want to carry out your father's desires. He was a murderer from the beginning, not holding to the truth, for there is no truth in him. When he lies, he speaks his native language, for he is a liar and the father of lies. (John 8:44, the Bible)

Daniella and I are both stunned to learn that when Apollyon, or as we know him, Michael, lies, he is speaking in his native language. We look at each other wondering who we are fighting. On second thought, maybe we can't handle that information right now.

The Meltdown

When April comes back from holiday, she is so angry that she starts to melt down. This is when it hit me: she was with June when she died. This fact alone is very weird as they were not even friends. She was the one sitting in June's apartment watching her suffer, I mean helping her. But helping her do what? She called 911 a little too late.

April begins to show signs of violence. She is very upset with the office, and she hates Michael for broken promises. Michael does not seem to care and keeps on working and making broken promises. I begin to keep my eye on Michael and April. To see why people are found dead with no explanation. Animals are disappearing, and we have no idea about that either.

Finally, after many months of torture and trying to fight with the office, April moves on to bigger and better things. The last couple weeks are the toughest as she will come to the window and do nothing but try to fight with me and Daniella. I refuse to give her what she wants. By this time, I am aware that unless I fight this evil in the spirit world, I can't win, and win I will. I have to win as the residents that are not evil depend on me. It is an exhausting battle. Every day she will try to bring me into her world of hate and unrest. I just won't bite. Then they discover she has cancer. Wow, shocker. I believe somebody that evil is so susceptible to diseases. She tries to pull me in with the cancer card. Again, I do not bite, and that infuriates her even more. I can pray for her without buying into her drama. To this day I do not know if she really has cancer or not, I only know she states she has to move to be closer to her doctors. One less evil being around. I must admit it is so hard to not get caught up in the drama. I like saying what I think. However, I realize that not every situation needs to hear what I think. After being silent on the matter for several days, which feels like several months, she leaves, and there is a type of peace in the land, for now.

Profiling

Working in the field of intelligence is a complex profession. I decided to get my next degree in profiling, or reading the darkness and the light in people. I know you are wondering where you go to get a degree like that. Profiling is a study of people and their behavior during a crime. While the criminals that I am profiling at this time may or may not want me dead, I still need the skills to determine which criminals will kill me and other residents. I needed to learn investigative techniques, interviewing techniques, and analyzing a potential witness. This is extremely important as many residents will say anything to set somebody up to take a fall. This scenario is also used to try and bring my staff and me down. I also have a lot of experience in playing mind games. Jack and Lucy were good at mind games, and my ex-husband was very good. Only one thing they did not count on was the student became better than the master. I was able to out think them and outwit them. This is very helpful in my current positions.

In most cases where I am concerned, if I turn my back on one of the residents, there will be a knife in it. My job is to study individuals' patterns, motives, and methods of the criminal. I must use all the evidence that I find to create a profile. In my case, the crime scene is this building. I have many suspects that I must eliminate by sending them to prison, evicting them, or ruling them out altogether. After I do this, then I can begin to work toward clearing the building of the more hardened criminals. Unfortunately for me, I must work to take down several suspects at one time. If I do not, then I won't last through this assignment.

I have two reasons I decided to expand my degree to include criminal profiler. The first reason was I wanted to know what made Jack and Lucy abduct me as a baby from my front yard, and I decided this would add to my living a while longer in my new reality. The

This Road is a Detour

first is for closure. I need to understand what drives a couple to take something that does not belong to them and then act like this was normal. I was one of the lucky ones as I was not tortured. I grew up in Hillbilly Hell. That only means that my dad did not want us to have a TV, indoor plumbing, or a phone. Food was on the scarce side since the good food was for the girls that spent the night. I remember that the only good meal I would receive would be on Sundays. For some reason, Jack thought Sunday was sacred, and therefore we should eat. We never questioned Jack as he was a very mean man at times. He would interpret our asking questions to mean we were talking back to him. In that case, we could find ourselves hit hard enough to go flying across the floor. I tried it once. I did not like it, so I just kept my mouth shut.

My mother, Lucy, grew up in the city with all kinds of amenities. Therefore we had a toilet, TV, and a phone that Jack sometimes paid for and sometimes did not pay for. He had money. We just don't know what he did with it. Maybe someday that mystery will be solved as well. Even with my mother growing up in the city, she would put up with him making food a luxury in Hillbilly Hell. It seems that the others, the girls that stayed for a night or two, always had plenty to eat, and I got what was left over. We did have a decent meal on Sundays. It was the only good meal of the week.

The second reason is obvious. When I go into a job like this, I can make a lot of enemies, and I never know who they are. The person you least expect to come after you is the one holding the gun. I must be able to discern and understand who is good and who is evil. While I have very strong intuitive and analytical skills, I'm still learning how to control my emotions. I can tell you this, once I'm done with a person, I'm done. I am reaching done with this maintenance person. The lies are mounting up, and he needs to get some work done. As I study profiling, I learn that people who lie will not be very trustworthy. You think?

I am alone because most people do not understand that to fight crime of this magnitude, you must fight it from every angle.

51

You can't always see the enemy. I must know how to outthink, outwit, and outmaneuver through the darkness of this world I now call my reality.

Michael/Apollyon

Apollyon has taken over Michael almost completely. Lies are normal for Michael, and he can't tell the difference between reality or lies. and to him it is the same thing.

He walks around telling everybody that he is in charge and that the office is a threat to everybody that lives in the building. He reminds them that as long as they obey him, they have nothing to worry about.

Just to be sure that Michael is in complete submission to Apollyon, he sends a woman to secure Michael's loyalty. She is cold, calculating, and everything Michael ever wants. She makes sure that Michael's soul is as cold as a dead fish. Okay, weird analogy, but funny. Isn't that the way it usually works, find the weakness and it can be used against you?

The only way that the property will be safe is with the head of the beast destroyed. Last year I was fighting Apollyon, and I received a slit in each eye (not at the same time) that would have been difficult. I was paralyzed for a while through a doctor that was on the side of the evil one, and my stress level was off the charts. One year later and I'm almost back to top speed. I fired the doctor and have found a new one. My eyes can see with no explanation of what happened. I need to be in the best physical, mental, and spiritual health I can be in to win this battle of wits. Most of the time it is all mental and you just must wait out your enemy.

Apparently, Apollyon doesn't remember that when fighting my last battle, I won. It was a close call, but I did win.

Daniella and I begin to study the mob and the overseers. Sometimes it is hard to tell them apart, except the overseers just want to torture me and Daniella.

Mob mentality

The gang of eight is slowly becoming the gang of twenty-eight. They talk to new residents, and they all form a hatred toward me then Michael, or at least that is what I think. Appearances can be deceiving. I would like to think that I have it all together and that I only trust those whom I should trust. That is not true. Sometimes I'm trusting, believing that deep down in there is good in most people.

The Gang Is an Angry Mob

According to *Flow Psychology*, mob mentality, also known as herd mentality, is a happening that describes how humans can influence each other. This type of mentality dates all the way back to the Salem Witch Trials that took place around 1692. I hope this mob is not thinking about burning me at the stake. Okay, that is a little dramatic. However, I will not put that past them. During the time of the witch hunts, if you weren't the hunted, you were part of the mob hunting and burning others. I would think from studying people and this gang, when you are pointing the finger at others, it takes the light off you.

Flow Psychology reports the Internet has become a breeding ground for this kind of behavior. A person can bully another person so easily on the Internet and shields the abuser under the anonymity cloak, which gives the individual freedom of letting go of the social restraints. Often a peaceful mob can be turned violet by the actions of a ringleader or two people forming a group. Social media also has different standards for different folks. This mob can write what they want, make a social media site, and run our name into the ground with nobody to bother them or take their actions to heart. On the other hand, if I write one religious or political thought, I could have my post taken down immediately. Hmm, are we seeing a pattern here? I've tried to have the bogus social media page the mob created taken down with no success at all.

We find this mob mentality a lot when a group is upset about something that has happened or they think in their minds has happened. They will connect with many other people across the Internet and start a huge protest. Most of the protesters have no idea what they are protesting, but they continue to loot and destroy a town or city anyway.

Usually, the bullying or mob mentality happens with several people who present the idea of belonging look attractive, and they usually target the weakest among the group. This idea is according to Tamara Avant, who is the psychology program director at South University, Savannah.

After reading all this, we hope to be better armed to tackle this problem.

Before we bury social media, we have to remember these people were taught this behavior long before social media was up and running. You find this mob mentality everywhere if you just watch people. Work, church, neighborhoods, and so on. Well, you get the idea. Just remember that little bully you went to grade school with is now grown up and probably still a bully. That is the problem. Now I must find the answer.

Officer Luke Smith

We have an incident where the police must be called. I think one of the residents is going to come right through the window at us. He is so angry because his rent has gone up by five dollars. Daniella is calm and tries to talk him down off the ledge. When she can't get him to comply, I call the police.

Officer Luke Smith shows up. He is just so cute. If I would have known about him before, I would have called the police a long time ago. He is tall. He is about six foot, dark black hair, and baby blue eyes. He has a beard that is salt-and-pepper. *Okay, stop staring*, I told myself. And those muscles, now he did not just wake up with them? I keep wanting to kick myself. "Victoria," Daniella says, "are you okay?" I answer, or try to answer, "I'm fine."

My face is red. My eyes are fixed on Officer Luke. What, am I in high school? I'm acting like I never saw a handsome, well-built man in a uniform before. Besides I'm in the witness protection program. I'm pretty sure that our Officer Luke will not find that attractive. Why am I even thinking about this? I'm the most undatable person here.

I'm staring again! Does he know that he is so good-looking that we are now going to have to find crime to be able to call Officer Luke back again and again?

At any rate, he takes the resident off in handcuffs, and the place has some peace again. Sometimes I feel like I jump from babysitter to director all in one hour. How does one get so angry over five dollars? It doesn't really matter. Just meeting Officer Luke makes the mess worth it. It is probably part of the gang's little plan, the angry part, not Officer Luke, who is so cute. If this gang thinks for one moment that I have one second of pleasure after meeting Officer Luke, I'm sure they would find a way to keep him away from our property.

Once we begin going through each of the members of this gang, we will find the weak spots and try to use the weakness against them. I know this sounds evil. but sometimes you must fight evil with head games. It is difficult because as we are trying to figure out how to isolate them, they are killing one another the entire time. They don't usually mess around. If they think you are a weak link, you are gone. The killing does not seem to affect them. Well, okay, it does affect the one they decide to kill off, but the ones doing the killing keep killing, eat supper, and have a good night's sleep. That is just cold. Nope, not turning my back on them. I'm not eating anything they provide, and any gifts they give us will be trashed as I'm sure they have poison, a recording device, or an evil spirit on the gift. This case is harder because there are so many to watch, take notes on, and protect us from.

Family Crisis

Just about the time I think I have moved from Hillbilly Hell and made a new life for myself, one of the kids shows up. Krista shows up complaining about how her life is a mess now that the other kids are in jail and her mother and father are in a retirement home. Krista always was a self-centered brat. Brat or not, here she is, and I can't let her get into my business. This distraction can get us all killed.

I try to be kind and ask her, in a nice way, "What do you want me to do?" She seems to have lost her direction since she is not taking orders from Mommy and Daddy anymore. I'm praying God will allow me to show kindness when all I want to do is send her back to where she came from. She asks if she can stay at my apartment for a while so that she can get her life together. I think about that for a moment. I inform her that she can stay for one week. After that, if she wants to stay in Oklahoma, she better find a job and a place to stay.

She agrees, and now I'm living with my past once again. Hopefully she really does want to bond with me. We will see. Tonight, we will keep it light and cheery.

In the meantime, I take her to the apartment so she can settle in for now. I'm still wondering why she is here. She never really treated me with too much kindness. Okay, so I question everybody. Now we know why I'm not married. I could change my mind with Officer Luke.

There is just something unsettling about Krista showing up right now.

Maintenance Evil on Steroids

This maintenance man always seems liked he is helping. At the time, I am grateful. Then later that week, the maintenance staff go to training for several days, and the truth comes flooding in. There is so much information I can hardly take it all in. At one point, my assistant, Daniella, and I are just speechless. Obviously, Michael is doing more than maintenance, and everybody is afraid of him. How can one person hold so much power over others?

The strong one, Michael, I notice, does all the talking for both him and Peter. What is that all about? When I hired Peter to replace Brandon, I really thought that he would work independently. As the week progresses, things only get worse. Michael will come into the office every ten minutes to see what we are discussing. No work is being accomplished because he is not getting any information to relay to the evil that is lurking outside in the lobby. Peter has to go as well because he seems to do Michael's bidding all the time.

Apollyon is always lurking around my office to see how he can get invited in. I try to tell the maintenance man that he needs to stop allowing the evil to take place on this property. My one superpower is discernment, and it is being taxed. I needed an ally in this war. I need to pray harder so that I will know just who that is. One thing I keep reminding myself is that God is not the author of confusion.

I now realize that the only person I can trust is Daniella. I began to talk with her about the evil in the apartment complex. She agrees that if we can remove the evil, we could relax a little. Thus, the removal process begins. This is like tearing a Band-Aid off a little at a time. However, I have learned that I must be patient so that I don't mess up God's plan, something that I am good at.

Seeing the Enemy

You can't always see the enemy. I must know how to outthink, outwit, and outmaneuver the evil in this world. Today a drug head decides to go off the deep end when he smoked some bad weed. He rips his clothes off and begins to go after the men outside on the apartment grounds. Where he got the stuff is what I must find out. That video is so hard to watch as a demonic group is enticing the group of women to laugh at the kid on the drugs. They are taking pictures of him and laughing like a bunch of crazed people. He is slithering around like a snake, and they are taking videos like it is funny. I want to puke, but that will show weakness, and the enemy looks for weakness of any kind. The guy that set him up is making him stay in the ring of onlookers so they can continue to laugh and take pics for social media.

Michael tries to talk to the kid so he can help him get on his feet. He will need to find a place to live so he will not have an eviction on his record. Or at least that is what I thought was happening. The kid has so much evil living in him at this time all he can do is laugh at this act of kindness. Which means in the end, the lies and the drugs will get him evicted, and he will be homeless.

The women are upset because they feel like they are being targeted and can be violated at any time. With laws the way they are today, somebody actually has to harm you before you can get any protection. Yet they will not write anybody up on a comment form because they are afraid of Michael. I finally find his weak spot this week. Now he is going down. I hate it when people pick on others that are weaker than themselves.

It might take a while, but I will get to the bottom of this situation. Thank God Daniella is strong and can stand with me. I don't know what I would do without her now that she is here. I was very tired and lonely at the end of the day because I did not have somebody around that thought like I did on this property. She is smart and knows her job well.

Bedbugs, Bugs from Hell!

Some of the residents don't seem to be able to shake off the bedbugs. I am at a loss so I will have to hire an outside agency to come in and spray for us.

The residents that wanted the outside agency to come in a spray wants that company to buy the bedbug covers for their bed. I realize they are all just freaking out. I too freak out when I think about bedbugs. At my last assignment residents were being killed by some kind of super bedbug. I never did find out what that was all about. There is just so much I can do at one time. I get annoyed with myself since I can't seem to fight more than one or two battles of evil at a time. I get tired at the end of the day.

Well I will end this, here and now. We will spray and the residents will buy their own covers. They can purchase them from the office and make payments on them if that is what they want to do. I will explain to them we don't have money to just purchase bedbug covers for everybody. If I buy for one, I must buy for all. Some understand this fact and some not so much. This bedbug thing has got to get under control. These are bugs from hell. They do not carry any diseases therefore the Center for Disease Control does not see them as a threat. However, they do make people go crazy. I feel like I'm a sane person, well okay as sane as can be expected, and I freak out over bedbugs.

This has been a day then again it really has been a month.

Did I mention I hate October? Why do all my enemies try to come out at once? Darkness tries to reign for one month anyway.

Bedbugs Again!

Here we go again with the bedbug issues. Are these people crazy, or do bedbugs just follow them around like bad luck or something?

Then again sometimes it is hard to tell when somebody just goes over the edge and loses it over something like bedbugs or they are making drama mountains out of drama hills. We had a resident once that was upset with the office, and he would not work with us to rid his apartment of the bedbugs. So one day he came to the window, and when we opened the window to see what he needed, he tried to flick the bedbugs in the office. Sometimes the only way to get rid of the little devils is to wrap everything in plastic wrap and throw it away. I'm talking about the stuff, not the humans. It is sad to see people lose everything. Then once you have them under control, you can do preventive maintenance on them. We quickly learned to drill holes in the walls and spray or powder the inside of the walls. This will stop them from spreading to other apartments. We tear back the baseboard and put bedbug powder down, then we glue the baseboard back on the wall. This also will help stop the little devils.

Once we were doing inspections, and we found that one of the residents had bedbugs in a jar like they were her pets. Really? How insane is that? Get a dog! Trust me, out here in the real world, there are a lot of insane people running around. You just don't know who they are. They say, whoever they are, that one out of every three people are crazy. In that case, look at your two friends, and if they are not crazy, it's you. Okay, I have no idea who said that or if it is even true, but it is a funny thought. This person, like most of our guests that stay with us, has issues.

I may have issues, but I try to hide them behind a face of sanity. Sometimes it works, and sometimes it does not work.

I go back to my desk and take a calming breath. I must be able to take it easy, or I'm going to let the enemy think I have weaknesses.

And right now, I have so many enemies that showing weakness is not an option. He fights dirty, and I must keep my guard up. The one way to take Michael out of the picture is find his weakness and work that angle. He so darn hard to understand. He jumps from light to darkness in a second. From crazy to sane in a matter of moments. Then he is so vague that I can't get a straight answer out of him. One time I ask him while making small talk what is the plan for the weekend. You would have thought I have just asked him out. He is stammering and being weird. It is a little funny to see how he hates being in my presence since he is morphing into an evil being. Once I learn I can make him jumpy, the game is on, at least for me.

Little do I know that while I am trying to find his weakness, he is robbing us blind. I'm not sure where that saying comes from. He is robbing us and taking complete advantage of us. He has a great little scam going on. The other thing I have learned about Michael is if it looks like a duck, or in this case a druggy, and it talks and walks like one, then it probably is one.

Michael's Weakness

Finally, I learned Michael's one weakness is his ego. The ego can really get in the way of things. In Michael's case, his ego is the super ego or his self-worth. When a man believes he is more important than God himself, he is in real trouble. Michael has been deceived into believing that inside this agency, he is the most important being here, and if he did not come to work, the residents will not be able to wake up in the morning safe.

Michael believes that it is because of his willingness to get work orders done, apartments are made ready to rent, and he controls the residents, the residents sleep easy at night. Even though he roams the halls trying to take their meds because he is addicted and he tries to get me fired daily. I'm not so worried about the firing part, but I am worried about the people who live here. I have my suspicion that some sexual abuse is going on as well, but I can't prove it.

His ego condemns him when he does not dress for success or get things done fast enough, so I cannot find fault with him at this time in these areas. His ego lets him believe all women need and depend on him and that weak men want him in ways that should not be talked about. He has a lie for everything you ask him. And he spills these lies to the elderly women that live here. Most of them have not had any attention paid to them, so when he comes into the apartment to do work orders, he pays them some attention, and there you have loyalty for life.

If your ego is always telling you what to do and how to do it, you are on a path that leads to destruction. Can we assume that this path then is not good but evil? In this story, we will call Michael Apollyon, which means "the destroyer." At first, I believed him. Then he produced a baptismal sheet to prove he was baptized. This action, of course, was to gain my trust. It is not real. It worked quite well for me as I went along with the document. We all have a shady past, but if we have a relationship with God, who was I to question his relationship? His God relationship was to make me trust him. He wanted me to believe that if he was praying and being a good person, I could in turn trust him. Wow! I was never so wrong.

Then I learned that in my case the only way he can get to me is in my dreams if I do not fall asleep naturally. Therefore, I must work until I am dog tired and fall asleep naturally and not pill-induced. If I fall asleep any other way, he will enter my dreamscape and terrorize me. This has happened only one time, and never again will I take a risk of falling asleep any other way than naturally. This makes me weak, and I cannot fight the next day. Michael can win that way and only that way. Otherwise, I am the stronger one of us. I stay prayed up, and that keeps me stronger. I get beaten up sometimes, but I will win the war.

My next game is to fight the ego. If I can control the ego, I can control the man. I learned this on Friday. However, it is dangerous to be alone with him when his ego is getting to be very large. I will prepare.

Preparing will take time. If Michael has no clue we are onto him, we should not have any problems. After all, he always wants all eyes on him in a good way. It is my job to make him believe that he is in charge. He will make a mistake! And we will give him what he wants: all eyes on him.

He hides a lot of things. Therefore, it is harder to control him. It is easier to fool him. He will believe anything that fills up the ego. The ego really can lead to a person's downfall. We must keep ego in check. Humble but strong. In Michael's case, he is so busy trying to use these old women that he has become shady and angry. His drug addiction and his need for the drink will win in the end.

Ego Training

Ego does not really exist. The ego must be fed. How to feed something that does not exist except in the spirit world? One must enter that world and send the message through the brain telling the receiver what they want to hear. This is also known as head games, something I am gifted with. In Michael's case, how important he really is to the mission at hand. The hardest part of this training is keeping your feelings intact. Michael is a very good maintenance person when he is walking in the light and not darkness. He has so much potential. The evil knows this as well.

When you think about it, we all have so much potential, and you can use that potential for good or evil. This will always be your choice. You can wake up each day and decide to serve in the darkness and evil or in the light. We have free will, and God allows us to use it. The only hard part for me is that Michael jumps from the dark side to the light so fast, and many times in a day that I have a hard time keeping up. I realize I already said that, but I have never encountered such an enemy that can jump for light to darkness in one reality and at a fast rate of speed. So in this case, I have to retreat, make sure I know the mission.

Feeding an ego can get tricky, especially for me. I am so straightforward that it is hard to play ego mind games. However, if I let him think he is in control, this builds and feeds his ego. He will make mistakes. If you believe you are more than you really are, then you do drugs on a regular basis, your success rate is not going to be high or last long. It always amazes me when a person cannot see this for themselves. While this is a hard concept for me to grasp, it makes for an interesting story, don't you think?

Family Interruptions

I'm calling it a night. After all, I have family at my apartment, and I must go home and deal with Krista. I'm tired, I'm hungry, and I don't want to deal with more emotion. I need a long shower and some food. Maybe Krista and I can watch a movie. I hope it is not too positive thinking that she can be somewhat normal and just chill. We will see.

Daniella reminds me to be careful and watch my back. We both get the office ready to lock up until we come back in the morning.

Once home, I try to make small talk with Krista, and that just does not work. She does not trust me, and I certainly don't trust her. What on earth is she doing here? Why is she staying at my home? Guess I will be sleeping with one eye open tonight.

She does, however, want to talk about my work. Now that is a first. Not much I can share at this point. Wonder why she is so interested. I really don't take her to be the law enforcement type. I will give her a small dose of my reality, then I'm going to inform her that she must leave before this gets too complicated.

Maybe things will look better in the morning. Life always looked better after a good night's sleep.

The Next Morning

As I wake the next morning, things do look better. Krista actually looks human and somewhat grateful for being in Oklahoma. Can I trust her? Probably not! She wants to come to work with me and help me clean up the office. I guess that is better than having her stay in the apartment all day going through my things.

We get up and get dressed. Then I explain to her that I need to stop at the local coffee shop so that I can caffeinate myself. Krista thought that is funny, but she jumps at the chance to have a coffee and a sandwich.

Once at work, the drama begins. Seems one of the residents died last night. I say *died* like it was a fall-asleep kind of died. Nope, not in this place. Seems several of the residents were fighting last night and yelling at this woman. She was very upset when she went to her apartment. It was around 3:00 a.m., and her neighbor heard a noise like she dropped something very heavy. Did the neighbor go and check on her? Heck no. The next day when her friends did not see her anywhere, they had us check on her. There she lay on the floor, and her coffee is spilled everywhere. Now I must call the police and I must fill an apartment. And I have more paperwork. Okay, that sounds a little cold, but I do not know this person, and apparently her friends did not care enough to check on her after they heard her fall. I hope she has some family. This gang of hate is infiltrating the entire building. Who lets somebody lay for hours without checking on them when they hear a loud noise that does not sound normal? These people do. Remind me not to get sick around here. I am clearly on my own. On second thought, I would have a lot of help only over the edge if they thought I was close enough to death without them being discovered.

After I get the facts of the drama, I turn around and notice that Krista is missing. Where has she gone now? I feel like I'm babysitting the entire world. I get it, these are my monkeys, and this is my circus. After this assignment is over, I need a vacation. And I know just the place. I'm going back to Harrah, Oklahoma, so that I can find my real family. The family that was stolen from me when Jack and Lucy decided to steal me out of my front yard when I was just a baby. Then I had the opportunity to grow up in Hillbilly Hell. Okay, back to reality. That is enough of remembering since I cannot address that heartache at this moment.

Where is Krista? I will just have to track her down on the cameras. At first, I hated sitting here and watching the cameras for things that happened. I'm getting better at watching the cameras. and it has become normal. Krista must be around here somewhere. I'm sure she did not run off with maintenance. Now there is a frightening thought. Will she and Michael gang up against me?

Time will tell! I just need to find at that little darling before she causes even more trouble for me and Daniella.

The Mission

The mission is to save the building. The building needs to be saved from the evil people that live in the building. While God does not save inanimate objects like buildings, I am using the building as a figure of speech. The building will mean that all the good people in the building need to be protected from this evil. I only hope there are some people left after I remove all the evil.

I am the damsel in distress that cannot save the building on my own. Today is the first day of the mission. My assistant is great. She plays the part well. Michael's ego begins to grow. I have a talk with him about the security of the building, and he is on it. His ego now is growing, which means he is talking and happy. For something that really does not exist in this world, it is not hard to manipulate, and it controls so many people.

Officer Luke is called in on the death that took place last night. How kind they refer to what happened as a death. "Guess what! It was a murder!" I wanted to shout. Officer Luke will think I am as crazy as the rest of them if I suggest such a thing. He smiles and wants to ask a few questions. While nothing will make me feel better than to talk to Officer Luke, I really have nothing to say in the matter. But the residents have a lot to say, and talk they do for almost an hour.

Officer Luke comes by the office once he has all the information he can gleam from our little residents. *How precious*, as I'm rolling my eyes. Darn, I thought I had the eye rolling under control. Officer Luke does not seem to notice, so I sit there staring at him. How did he get so, well, you know, handsome? And kind. He always has a smile on his face. He probably does not have as much paperwork to do as I do. Just kidding, I'm sure he has some paperwork, and he just does it as he is smiling. I must work on my attitude. I really do love my job. It's people that I can get tired of.

Now where is Krista? I must find her so I can be sure she is not getting into trouble. Why do I always feel like I am responsible for everybody?

Back to the Mission

If I am not manipulating Michael for the good of the building, then the enemy is going to use him for his purpose, which is evil. He will use him to buy, sell, and use drugs. He will tell him he is worthless unless he is taking drugs and will not be able to keep up with all the work that needs to be done. While the enemy and I fight for this one soul, other people walk around like nothing is going on because the ones that identify with Michael currently have already lost their souls. The ones that have a living soul that belongs to the good side.

I become aware that while I am taking a mental health day, go ahead and laugh, but sometimes I just need a quiet day off, which we call our mental health day, Michael is carrying around a bag of candy. They call him the candy man when I am gone, and now, I know why he has earned that name. Drugs!

As it turns out, I battle well until the end. I can battle well, until I get tired, then the enemy can always hit me the hardest at the end of the day. Turns out our spy group has grown by one. I'm sure this shocked the enemy. One of the residents will rather keep the comfort of their home than fight for the enemy. Good choice! I will take that small victory.

She comes to us to share some much-needed information. We, my assistant and I, assure her that if she watches and reports, we will not assume she is a part of anything that Michael is a part of. I guarantee her she is doing the right thing by coming forward. Daniella, on the other hand, she is like the mafia threatening her never to be part of what the maintenance men are up to. Either way, it works, or we gain one more for our side. I can see the enemy seething at this point.

Unfortunately, during the day, many crazy people show up, and I'm worn-out in my mind and spirit by the time 4:30 p.m. comes. I begin to fight in my flesh, and that does not work very well. After a good night's sleep, I'm back in the spirit again, so I will text Michael to see if he will come in at 7:30 a.m. so we can prepare for today. I will go in at 7:00 a.m. so I can pray over the office that way the enemy can only listen in. Hopefully Michael will be able to stay in the office and talk to me. He has been very uncomfortable lately.

Now where is Krista so that I can get out of this place? I told her we would leave at 5:00 p.m. She is always so hard to find.

On the way home, Krista is asking all kinds of questions. I pray for a moment, then it hits me. She is trying to extract information out of me. Wow! She should know better I'm the professional here. However, now that I know what she is doing, maybe I can play along and find out who put her up to this and why she is siding with them and not me.

Once the weekend begins, I go to my whiteboard and start to think. It is the only way I can rationalize what has happened throughout the week. I'm not so sure I believe the resident that just came to the office scared she was going to lose her apartment because she was being lumped into the group with Michael and the rest of the druggies. I don't really trust anybody in this building right now. And it does not help much that medical marijuana is legal and now open carry is legal without a permit. All I can say is, "This is not my circus, and these are not my monkeys." Okay! Maybe this is my circus, and these are my monkeys. I must watch these videos one more time only slowly. I am missing something. I just know I am. Can you just imagine a bunch of crazy people hopped up on marijuana and carrying a gun? Yeah, I can't either.

Wait, there it is! That guy that smoked the bad weed, Tom, was set up. The two women paid the guy to take Tom off the property to get him high, then he brought him back to the smoke shack and threw him in the middle of the room like an experiment. I saw the women hand the kid money for getting Tom high. After further studying the tape, I realize Tom was the victim, and they were more than happy to let him take the fall. I just know Michael had a hand in this. I just need to find out how.

After much prayer and advice from the council that I trusted, I brought Tom, Michael, and Daniella into my office. We all talk about what should happen next. I tell them Tom will stay and that I will make a few calls stating I am still collecting evidence and that we will reschedule for a later date. Once I do this, the games begin. I warn Tom to be very careful. I know the three demons that came after him will be looking to come after him to kill him. If we can keep Tom alive long enough for me to plant enough doubt into the minds of these demons, they will destroy one another and Tom will be free. I can only pray that Tom will be safe until then.

My only worry is that people can manipulate Tom quite easily. He does not have the mental capacity to make wise choices. I'm hoping I can get to the bottom of this before he makes another bad choice. He just wants to be part of the group, and sometimes he will do whatever is asked of him to be part of that group.

Blindsided

Today is interesting as I am working at my desk trying to get caught up. We just survived an inspection, and we are preparing for another one. The tasks that keep our building afloat sometimes can be daunting. We are preparing for inspections, while Daniella and I watch our back and our office for any incoming demons that are following the orders of Apollyon.

Blindsided by Apollyon, whom we know is the evil one, comes in different forms. Today I was walking the halls talking to some of the residents when one of the evil spirits came by and scratched my eye to the point it was quickly becoming infected with a kind of foreign matter. Why is it always my eyes? Doesn't this monster have any more of an imagination than that? I have been given eyes that are strong meaning. I can discern things with my eyes most people cannot. Now this scratch healing will be time-consuming, but it should not last forever. If it does not heal quickly, I will go to the eye doctor. That should be fun. I can hear the questions now. How did this happen? Where were you to get foreign matter in your eye? Why is the eye so scratched? Does it itch and that is why you felt the need to scratch it?

One week later and it does not heal. I have to go see the doctor. The pain is a 10 by the time I do get to the doctor. The look on her face is priceless. She has the look of horror. She tells me, "I've had grown men in here with less of a cut in their eye and they were screaming." Okay! When did it go from a small scratch to a deep cut? I guess I have a high tolerance of pain. She just looks at me and smiles.

The doctor usually does not have a sense of humor when I just say, "No, I did not scratch my eye, and I have no idea how this happened." This is the third time this year. When she sees my eye, she is shocked. All right now, let's stop looking at the chick with the cut in her eye. She just repeats her previous statement, "I've seen grown men with eyes that are slit like this and they are crying." I just want it fixed so I can go back to work. It does hurt like crazy, but I have a high tolerance for pain. Didn't I just say that? I feel like I'm in one of those movies where everything gets repeated. She gives me some medicine and tells me to keep my glasses on. She recommends that I wear some type of glasses whenever I am out of my office. I smile and say, "Okay." What I was thinking was, "You think?"

As I work through the things that are happening at this complex, I try as hard as I can to figure out what is next. When does this stop? I will have to find better protection when I leave my office. They are always waiting outside the office, Apollyon and his crew.

I miss my whiteboard. When I write things down, it is much easier to see them. Okay, I can only half see right now, and I should rest my eyes, but I want to figure this out so I can solve this crime and go on vacation. It doesn't matter. I can't bring the whiteboard out until Krista is gone.

Now that I can't work anymore at home until Krista is out on her own, I suppose I will rest while at home. With Krista around, I must sleep with one eye open anyway. In this case, I will rest the eye that has the cut, and I will keep the good eye open. Doesn't sound too hard, does it? I think she is trying to be friends with some of the residents, not good! The next thing you know she will be plotting behind my back. She must go and soon. If I am going to die, it will not be at her hands. I lived and survived Hillbilly Hell. She won't get me now.

When does this stop? Now I live with Krista, and I feel like evil is all around me. I must find a happy place to have some peace.

First, I need to figure out the evil around me. Who is evil, who is not. Then I need to find the happy, peaceful place to rest during the day even for just one hour so I can refocus.

Levels of Evil

As we begin our work to remove and destroy the evil, we have learned that there are several layers of evil. It is like peeling an onion one layer at a time. And sometimes it does make us cry.

Level 1

This is the level that makes you wonder if the evil is real or perceived. The spirit at this point is usually kind to your face and evil behind your back. You only see what is on the surface of the evil. I have learned that to defuse the evil at this level, I just smile and keep my mouth shut. I have also learned over the years of fighting this type of evil, if you don't say it, they don't know about it. I try to keep my mouth shut. Do I always? No! Sometimes I get so upset that my emotions will take over. That is when I know I need a break. Time to regroup. I take a day off here and there to keep my mental, physical, and spiritual strength intact. That is why it is important to find a happy place to retreat to during the day when I need it. The hardest thing for me is keeping my mouth shut and my eyes from rolling. Seems as soon as I try to keep my mouth shut, my eyes begin to roll. I'm not sure if they are connected in my brain or not, but if one isn't working, the other seems to step up and work just fine. Daniella, on the other hand, is a rock. Nobody can tell what she is thinking or what her emotions are. I'm so glad she is on my side.

The gang of hate is at the level 1 currently. I am still working on getting to know them. Some of them appear to be eviler than the others. I'm not sure evil is something you can measure as in this person is eviler than that person. It just seems that way. I have been told that they prey on the weak, and if the weak don't comply, they will kill them. I must identify the gang members from the victims, and sometimes it is hard to tell which is which at this level of evil. I

78

am beginning to believe the rumors that if the weak don't comply, they will die, as several people have mysteriously died since I have been here.

Level 2

This level is the level of casting a light on the darkness. Once this happens, the evil will hide. Most of the evil currently is gossip, and it is everywhere. I just need to cast the light and see who is running. It reminds me of turning on a kitchen light and watching the roaches run. Sounds gross, I know, but that is about how it works with these guys as well. At this point, Michael is the only one that has me confused as he can jump from darkness to light and back to the darkness so quickly. And he is the father of lies. As we learned in Sunday school, Satan is the author of lies. That will make Michael Satan or Satan is Michael. It is hard to keep up with the lies and the jumping from light to dark so quickly. Michael or Satan, whoever knew what state of mind he would be in? Once Michael begins doing drugs and drinking, he is more guarded. However, in this state of mind, he makes more mistakes. That is why I give him the name Apollyon, which means "destroyer, Satan, Father of Lies." I continue to cast a light in the darkness wherever I can. This makes the evil extremely irritated. On one occasion they were so mad at me they scratched my eye, and did it ever hurt. This was the other eye. Either I'm glad I only have two eyes to scratch or I'm wondering what else they can hurt. When I finally made it to the doctor, she just gasped at the gash. Whoever stated fighting evil would be easy has not had a good fight.

So much evil, so little time.

Shining light on evil can be easy. It is dealing with the outcome that is difficult. The textbook answer to shining light on evil is easy. It only takes a smile, an act of kindness, or just listening to somebody who is lonely. And since I took classes on listening, that helps me in these times of evil encounters. Smiling is not difficult for me, and doing an act of kindness is not that difficult unless it is one of the little monsters. I always try to break through the evil in them before I kick them out the door. I do believe everybody deserves a chance.

Smiling is a great way to get people to soften up. However, at times an evil person will try to match wits with me. I usually win. Good always wins in the end.

So the next time you see level two evil, try a smile or a kind deed to overcome the evil.

Level 3

This is the holy level, or should I say unholy level. The last level. It exposes the darkness for you to see exactly who you are dealing with. When you arrive at this level, things are starting to make sense. The pieces of the puzzle begin to fall into place. You begin to realize the strategy that you need to be able to fight this evil and win. It takes patience and it takes strength to make it to this level. I only learned this through the fights that I have been in. If I move too quickly, then I cannot hear or see what to do to win. This is the hardest part. I like to act quickly sometimes, and then I miss what is happening. When this happens, I usually pay the price of being attacked and losing. In my case, some part of my body is usually attacked. Trust me, fighting evil like this is a lot harder than fighting any gang on the border. I miss my border patrol days. I miss Cindy's Place, where girls could go and find a new start away from the gangs. Sometimes we would send them to another state or just keep them close where we could keep an eye on them. In all my time fighting crime at the border, I was never confused about who was the enemy or was not the enemy. And gangs had an honor code of such. If you broke the code, you would be dead. That is how I ended up fighting crimes in the FBI witness protection program. Now that I'm here, I wonder which is the safest place border or apartment complex. Say what you want about the gangs, but most of them were not plain crazy. These criminals at this complex will kill you then go have lunch. No conscience whatsoever. When dealing with people who only have one agenda, theirs, it can be hard to weed them out. It takes patience and hard work.

Yes, I see (well, only half see until my eye heals) a vacation in my future.

Two Leave and More Come!

Just when you think that you are jumping ahead of the evil, more evil shows up. I've been watching several of them. They creep around trying to be friends with others. The others are always somebody weaker than themselves. Sometimes it works, and sometimes it is just wasting everybody's time. They work best in groups. If they can't allure others to follow them, then they try to cause so much trouble for the person they are targeting that the target usually leaves. That is why this gang is so dangerous. They are all bullies and very self-serving. Apollyon is not stupid. He likes to keep them grouping together like a mob, then it is harder to control from my end. Sometimes it is better to just ignore them, and then they get frustrated and move away. Some move out, and some just move to another part of the building. They may move away, but it is not forever. Apollyon always has a group that wants to disturb the peace of others. Funny when they lease in, you would never know they are that evil. Some of them are not evil until they are taken in by the gang.

We still do not know who the leader is and which resident is carrying out the leader's orders at any given time. I have my suspects.

Donna is the most evil and high on my suspect list. She can smile in your face then turn around and stab you and the person who is standing with you at the same time. She also has a cousin who resides at the property, and we believe that Donna is trying to poison her with some kind of drug that makes the cousin hallucinate. Her cousin Sarah would come to us and ask us to spray for the bugs that would eat into her food and into her skin. We went up to her apartment several times and did not see anything. We sprayed once or twice. She would get so mad at us because we did not see the bugs. Then we began to notice a pattern. When Sarah was going out to eat, she would start to feel normal and talk with people around her. Once this would happen, then Donna would begin to take care of

Sarah, and she would start to hallucinate. All we could do was watch because we could not prove anything, and these people are all so tight-lipped they would not tell on one another. I guess it is the fear factor that keeps them from telling what they know. I will find out what they know, or I will eliminate them from this complex. Sooner or later evil always slips up, and then we can evict them.

Crow

Crow lives in apartment D204 and is very high on my suspect lists. This man is so full of hate that you can actually see it coming out of his body. The hate and the evil have contoured him so badly it is hard to look at him. He fits the profile of a maniac as he does not come out of his room except at odd times. He is small in body size and does not appear to be very threatening at first glance. One would think because he is so skinny, he would not hold much power over these people. His way of keeping the office occupied is calling the authorities on us. I've never known so many different agencies existed. We never know who will show up that day to investigate us. I learn a lot of apartment management skills from good old Crow. He comes out of his apartment long enough to stir up the crowd, then he goes back in his room and sit. Why do they listen to him? I will never understand why they follow the evil around like they do.

He is furious one day because he does not like the food that we serve for Christmas dinner. As if he has a say! Then he turns us in because we will give away toilet paper and other necessities people needed at the end of the month. Most of these people have little income and we are just trying to help them. Most of our residents do not have families that visit them or help them in any way. No, helping others is not going to happen while Crow is here. He stops the giveaways quickly. Even giving away the essentials that people need. All our giveaways are donated, and we want to pass on the kindness.

Next, he complains because he does not like our seasonal decorations. He states they are too childish. Like he would know what is childish and what is not. After all, he is acting quite childish. It is at this time I start to ignore him. He is never going to be satisfied, so who cares what he thinks? It is also at this time he begins to get others evicted, then he will call Fair Housing on us. What a circle of deceit.

When he isn't busy complaining, he will plant things to give us the reasons we needed to evict him. Once the eviction process begins, he takes us to court. Once the court battle is over, which ends up being three to six months' worth of battle and several thousands of dollars later, he finally leaves. It is at this time I want to dance in the streets for the victory I am feeling. I also learn not to celebrate too soon. When one evil person leaves, it feels like there are ten more that show up to replace him. The dancing stops.

June

Now here is a piece of work. I did not know at the time I began my work at this complex that she was the head of the complex, and she did think she ran the place. Okay, she did run the place when I got there. She was approximately eighty years old, and did she ever have spunk. She was about four feet tall, and the power she felt she had was a story in itself. I remember she never smiled. She was very negative. On one occasion, she was having a birthday. I tried to make friends with her by giving her a bag of goodies. As she pulled each one out, she had some negative remarks. As she did this most of the stuff, I took from her and threw it in the trash can. Once our little display of rudeness was over, I closed the trash bag and promptly took it to the trash can. And that was the end of that. The look on her mean face, priceless!

I tried to use the school of thought, that is, keep your friends close and your enemies closer. If we were in a normal situation, this would have worked. This is not a normal situation. She ended up being much stronger than I would have thought. She was also a CI (confidential informer) for the board of directors, which I did not know about. No wonder every time we had a meeting, they would line up waiting to go into the meeting so they could try to hang me with something. June was always trying to stir something up. I've never had to go into battle with so many evil people at one time.

At first it was easy to let June run the show because it took some of the burden off me. I just did not realize people were so afraid of her. My gift of reading people needs to be sharpened if I am going to make it through this assignment.

I'm shocked that Michael did not help them. Then again, I guess he did behind the scenes. What is the definition of normal so we can compare it to this group of bullies.

Maybe we should take a moment to define *normal*.

Normal: Dictionary.com

normal
[nawr-m*uhl*] SHOW IPA
    SEE SYNONYMS FOR *normal* ON
THESAURUS.COM

adjective
    conforming to the standard or the common
type; usual; not abnormal; regular; natural.
    serving to establish a standard.

Psychology.
    1.   approximately average in any psycholog-
          ical trait, as intelligence, personality, or
          emotional adjustment.
    2.   free from any mental disorder; sane.

Biology, Medicine/Medical.
    1.   free from any infection or other form of
          disease or malformation, or from experi-
          mental therapy or manipulation.
    2.   of natural occurrence.

So according to dictionary.com, if you are normal, you are sane, free of mental disorder. Okay, that eliminates most of the people here at this complex.

Bullies really have no agenda except to divide and conquer, or in this case control. The control is the only thing they really want. Think of a mob that ebbs and flows together and cannot function unless they are sucking the life out of good people. It's like a blob of people that just look for any reason to stop the good so the evil can grow and take over. I'm sure if we go back into the past of these people, you would find out they were bullies in school when they were growing up. June and one of her sidekicks that followed every one of June's commands had keys to every apartment in the complex. People were so afraid that they were going to enter the apartment and kill them that they would never say a wrong word against June. This was one of the hardest evil people to take down. Then one day when I least expected it, she died.

I was so in shock to find out she died. Apparently her guts just exploded. At least that is what I heard. I heard later that April was with her when she died. That was so weird because they did not appear to get along. I never could figure out what April was doing in June's apartment when her guts exploded and the ambulance did not get there in time to save her. If your gut explodes, can you really be saved, and what causes your insides to explode? That is sure a story to tell the grandchildren.

Once she was dead, the family chose to have her cremated with no memorial service. It was odd as they did not seem to care if she was gone or not. What a sad commentary on one's life.

Jane was one of the followers. She would do whatever June told her to do. She also complained a lot. She hated to work, she hated our lunches, and she hated gifts from the office for her birthday and Christmas. In short, she was one hateful and miserable person. She was finally complaining one too many times, and I had to open my big mouth. Sometimes I just don't know what is going to come out of my mouth. I worked for five years to gain some kind of Holy Spirit control over what I say, and then bam! Out of nowhere, I just speak my mind, and it is not always pretty.

Jane was complaining about the lunch we had for a training session we had, and I told her not to let the door hit her on the way out if she could find a better opportunity, take it! She was so shocked that anybody would ever talk to her that way. As I heard a man once say, "It is what it is!" And life will continue.

April

April is a character that is hard to imagine. April has a very strong personality. She can seem very normal at any given time. Then in a minute she can jump into the darkness. This is the way Michael works as well. She has mental problems, and if Michael is not upsetting her, she is fine. Of course, Michael knows this, and he uses her mental issues to get her to hate the office staff. Because she has trust issues, and she has mental issues she begins to break down and a war inside of her begins to rage.

April has long blond hair, which is attractive to Michael. She is tall and a wee bit plump. She has a smile that shows off her beautiful teeth. She can be sweet, and she can be evil. One never knows who will show up on any given day.

As the rage in April continues, this is when she became friends with June, or maybe she was friends with her from the beginning at this point it is hard to know. June always appeared to be in charge, or at least she is allowed to think this. One thing I have learned about evil is if you stand back and pray then watch the outcome, they usually will eat their own. This was not the exception to the rule. They would hang out together at night. Evil always comes alive at night. They love the darkness, believing that the night darkness hides their wicked plans.

This went on for days that ended up being weeks. Michael, of course, kept pushing April. I begin my prayers to remove evil from this complex, seen and unseen. Michael always stirs the pot by promising the moon to all these women, then he does not follow through. This will infuriate some of them, and others will complain. I keep praying for the removal of the evil. Then after a couple of years it begins to happen, the removal begins. At times even I am surprised who can't stay.

In the manual, it states that Satan, Apollyon, goes around the earth seeing who he can devour. Not only that, he is the author of lies, killing, stealing, and destroying. Michael has just become that person right before my very eyes. Daniella and I could not believe the transformation. His eyes glaze over for just one moment, and they turn red. He is hissing, but I can't make out what he is saying. Once I realize what has happened, I choose not to say a word while he is around. This makes him so angry that we do not see him for the rest of the day. That is just fine by me. I feel like I take such a beating in some of these battles.

The Goliath Effect

Daniella and I begin to pray and prepare for battle as Michael, now full of many demons, will not be able to trust us. He will, however, make a mistake. I call it the Goliath effect! The bigger they are, the harder they will fall. This effect is led by the ego. Goliath believed that because he was so large and so strong not one Israelite was going to defeat him and then he would conquer the Israelites.

There was a man named Goliath who emerged to taunt the armies of Israel and challenge them to send their best warrior into the valley to fight (1 Samuel 17:8–10). The Bible tells us that this went on for forty days with no Israelite daring to step forward to face the fearsome giant (1 Samuel 17:16). That is, until David arrived on an errand from his father and sized up Goliath for himself.

The Masoretic Text, written in Hebrew, tells us he was six cubits and a span, roughly nine feet, six inches. The Septuagint, the ancient Greek translation of the Old Testament, says Goliath's height was four cubits and a span, about six feet, six inches tall. The Hebrew text found in the Dead Sea Scrolls tells us that Goliath was four cubits tall, which is about six feet. We can assume then that Goliath was at least six feet tall or a bit taller. He was well-built and well-trained in military skills.

Goliath donned a smorgasbord of military equipment—his greaves (a type of leg armor) were commonly worn by Aegean cultures, his helmet was like that of the Assyrians, his scale armor was akin to Egyptian armor, his sword was likely similar to an Eastern scimitar.

Imagine putting a thirty-pound weight on top of your head. That's about would be like to wear Goliath's helmet, which was basically a bronze bucket.

Now add to that a T-shirt that weighs about 150 pounds, a bronze-scaled coat of mail weighing in at five thousand shekels. That's like walking with a person strapped to your chest.

Throw on the ancient warrior equivalent of soccer shin guards (greaves), also made of bronze. Good luck running in those.

If that doesn't have you laying on the ground beneath the weight yet, it's time to add some weapons.

Now picture yourself carrying a massive walking stick made of bronze with a giant, pointy iron tip, a spear weighing around thirty pounds total.

Goliath also carried a magnificent sword (which David used to decapitate him). David kept this sword and took it later when he fled from Saul, saying, "There is none like it."

This is the same affect that Michael has. He believes because he can charm women and bully others that he is in total control. It is best to let him believe this so he becomes at peace and in charge. This will lead to mistakes, and when he makes a mistake, as all evil does, I will be there to catch him. Once I catch him, he is coming down.

Goliath made the mistake of thinking a little boy with a rock could not defeat him. It was not the fact that David fought well. It was the fact that he believed and had a large faith.

So here we are. I am going to have to have a faith and allow God in his timing take this guy down. Okay, I will have to fight hard as well.

Why do so many people have to go to the dark side? There must be something that I am missing. This guy must be getting something out of all this. He can't just be evil for the sake of being evil. Most humans want some kind of result. You know, like end satisfaction.

Now where is Krista so we can go home for the evening? What does she do all day long? I'm going to have to start following her with the cameras to see who she has become friends with. One more enemy, just what I needed.

Once in the car, I try to talk to Krista to find out what she had been up to. She is so vague then she gets a little put out with me. I'm beginning to think her stay with me is going to have to end sooner than later.

One Huge Battle
Lesson Learned!

The next day Krista is ready to leave and go to work with me without any resistance. That is odd. I'm wondering why she is so excited about going to work. I will keep a closer eye on her. Great, just what I need, one more person to watch.

The best plan that God has given me to date is to not show my hand. One of Michael's little demon buddies knows how to push my buttons, so it is hard to keep my cool. He has set me off three times now. What the heck is wrong with me? This guy can stand at that window, smile, and start to make my spirit show anger. He has called the newspaper about me, the city government about me, and who knows what is next. So now I will take a much-needed day off so that I can regroup. My next meeting with this little demon, I will be tough, and I need to be ready. If I can remove this man with all these demons from this property, we might be able to start healing. The Bible verse of the day is, "All things work together for the good of those who love the Lord" (Romans 8:28).

I feel like every time I meet this person, I'm angry, and I get set off. How do I compose myself? Lucky for me, Daniella can withstand him. For some reason, he does not set her off. He doesn't even mind talking with her. What is up with that? I'm not upset. I'm just shocked. Goes to show you when you are told you are in charge, that doesn't necessarily mean a thing. Most of the time I feel like the battle is personal when I'm trying not to let that happen. Truth be told, I am thankful Daniella can handle Sam and his outbursts.

So what does Sam gain by upsetting me? And who is pulling his strings? It is probably Michael. Once in a while, when Michael shows his good side, I really pray he will choose the good and straight path. I guess it is easier to follow the dark side. We will see. I used to be able to talk to Michael, and I thought he was listening. At least he had all the right answers. From what I could tell, he was telling me what I wanted to hear. Just like I am assuming he tells his wife and his girlfriends what they want to hear. This guy is really a piece of work.

Next Up, Demon Sam

This demon we already talked about. Sam came to us sad and distraught over the fact that his best friend just moved, his mother just died, and he lost his job. After Daniella and I discussed Sam's situation, he appeared to be a good choice to hire as a part-time custodian. We just wanted to help him become a successful person. Believing this would help him feel better about himself. Once he was hired, we had the shock of a lifetime. He began to be crazy. Right about here, I would usually say, "Act," but I don't think he was acting. I tried writing all his instructions down so that he would understand them, and he would give them back at the end of the day with all these weird writings on them. It was just bizarre. We tried everything to help this guy. We actually told him all he had to work was three hours a day thinking that was the problem.

We began to watch old Sam when we would come in in the mornings. After a few days, we began to see a pattern.

Sam's Termination

Termination sounds final, and while I wish he was off my property, I'm not going to kill him. I'm going to fire the little imp. I'm sure he will not take this sitting down, or maybe that is what he wanted all along. Sam always states, "I never quit my jobs." Guess he was telling the truth. He gets himself fired. I can't spend much more time trying to help somebody who does not want to be helped and is controlled by Michael, our destroyer.

Once I remove this threat. Michael will be easier to catch. He won't be giving Sam ideas on how to destroy Daniella and me as Sam will be neutralized. Sam will then become a nonissue to my building, my work, and my life. I like the sounds of Sam being neutralized. Could not happen to a better person. Let's see how Michael responds to this new twist in his life.

We will have to change lock combinations on two floors so that Sam will not be able to get into them. One of my wiser choices, when I decided to put combination locks on the doors so that we could easily change the numbers when somebody was fired.

Now to find Krista, I need a day off to summarize the situation and talk to Krista about moving on.

I always cherished my days at home looking at my whiteboard cooking a healthy meal and thinking. Not today, I get to spend it with Krista. Weird, but she wants to talk to me. Now I know why. She is asking all kinds of questions about the things that are happening at the apartment complex. Why is she so interested? Who is she hanging with at work? It is time to find out. I am having a great conversation with her, giving her all kinds of misinformation. Once she is satisfied, I decide I need some kind of relaxation. I decide to pull up a chick flick, get some chocolate, and zone out for a while. Then in the morning I will feel better. It just works that way. I think it is the chocolate. If I don't figure this thing out with Krista, I'm going to start shopping.

The next day we are up and ready to go. Today is the day I watch Krista now that her pretty little head is full of wrong information. I want to see where she goes and whom she is talking to. Once I do that, I will get firmer about her leaving.

Once a body is infected with the demons, it is almost impossible to help them. This particular person, Michael, stated he had been baptized. My first question is, baptized with what? Does the thought of many demons running through our churches bother anybody but me? Michael gets his baptism and goes on to be more evil than he was when he started his little charade. I must hand it to Apollyon. I did not see this one coming. The battle is starting to get intense. Now all I need is for Michael and Krista to team up. That would be one evil team. Will not happen. I will remove her first.

I watch Krista, and just as I thought, she is talking with the gang of haters. Of course we don't know if this is the group that she is talking to. They talk for a long time. It is so funny you can warn people and warn them about the cameras and they still forget.

I must retreat so that I know how to execute my next plan.

As I rest, I try to go over everything we do know and what we need to know. This is where my wipe board comes in. The sad part is this process works so much better at home, but I had to move the wipe board to my back office so Krista would not see it. What do we know? Michael believes he is in control. Every person that has been given a little power when they have never had power before lets it go to their head. In Michael's case, his ego is beginning to get out of control. He will stop at nothing to destroy the office and the rules and regulations the office stands for each and every day. He will try to destroy whatever stands in his way.

Michael Lies and People Die

He will lie to my face and believe the lie even when he is presented with evidence. He steals and kills. He has been warned to stay away from certain people who are weaker than he is. He does this only until I take off then he goes after them. Since I need to rest at times, I must trust they will make it through his attacks. Luke is one of my concerns. He has become my informant; however, he is weak. He has a girlfriend that lives with him now, and she appears to be stronger than Michael is.

As Daniella and I sit and talk over lunch, we hear a very loud noise. We finish our lunch then go to investigate. A dead body was wrapped in a carpet and dumped in the trash. Of course it is on the floor where the cameras don't always work. Daniella offers to call the police. I'm secretly praying that it is Officer Luke. He is so darn cute. Yes, the Yankee version of handsome is cute.

Once Office Luke arrives, we begin to interrogate the gang. They always act so cold like nothing ever happened. Donna is one of the coldest people I have seen in a long time. She just smiles and answers the question like she doesn't understand what all the fuss is about. This chick has got to go before anybody else dies. Now the police are talking to Michael. That should be good. He lies about everything, and everybody believes him. We are watching this all happen on camera. I will never really know what Michael lies about because he won't give me the same version he gives the police. He really needs to go too, but I would rather put him into jail than fire him.

Back to the carpet killer, that is what I will refer him or her to as we have a variety of suspects at this time. The rumor mill is a great place to start. Yes, it is the rumor mill, but I am smart enough to know that within every piece of fiction, there lies a bit of the truth.

And as we always say in the office, "You can't make this stuff up." It is up to us to figure out what is fiction and what is truth.

Seems Patsy was having sex with Michael and he was taking her drugs that she kept in a paper bag on her coffee table. He would run into the apartment have quick sex, and she would give him the drugs. Now this is becoming quite obvious, that Michael protects the ones he likes, and the ones he does not, he tries to have evicted.

Some of the gang members finally figured this out. So they tried to take Michael down, but he was too strong for them and had a few more smarts than they did. The next best thing was to kill his little buddy Patsy. Now all I must do is prove it. Michael really liked Patsy because he could control her. But even best friends are disposable in this place of horrors.

My only problem is that we cannot prove her death was done by one of the gangs since the cameras went down for a while during this time. Which means either Michael is part of the gang or he just jumps in and out of them as he desires. Now Officer Luke comes to the conclusion the Patsy's death is suspicious to say the least. You think? Oh no! His cuteness is now turning into stupidness. I can't help myself! I must ask the question. "Officer Luke, let me get this straight. What you are saying is, you do not think it is normal operating procedure for anybody to kill an old lady, wrap her up in a carpet, throw her down the trash bin?" He is just staring at me. Why is he just staring at me? Okay, I will bite, so I ask, "What is next?" He looks at me like I'm the crazy one around here. Then he finally says, "I will take all of this information back to my boss, and we will be in touch."

Oh brother, and to think I wanted to go out with this guy that is nothing more than eye candy. He is acting like the scarecrow off the *Wizard of Oz*. We are back to Michael's lies (about everything), and people die.

Krista

Now where is Krista so I can go home and get some rest? Tomorrow has to be better, right?

Time to go home and have it out with Krista.

On the way home, we are silent. We pick up supper from my favorite fast-food place. After all, if I'm going to war with somebody, I should have a meal I will enjoy. Or do I have that all wrong if I'm going to bring this evil person down, should they have their last supper? Oh, either way, I need have a good supper before I get into it with her. We still do not talk.

Once home, we eat in silence, of course. Then I begin to talk to her. "Krista, you cannot continue to go to work with me and hang out with my enemies. We have talked about this before. I think it is time you will need to find a place to live and soon. I'm done!"

She is clearly upset with me, and I think she blames me for Patsy's death. Of course she does that is what the rumor mill is saying. Time to set her straight. "Look," I begin, "I had nothing to do with Patsy's death. If you are going to continue to disrupt my peaceful enjoyment, then you will need to leave. In the morning, I want you out of my home and on your way." Okay, that is a shocker, even for me. I'm not usually that blunt. Once I recover from my bluntness, I try to talk her down off the wall because I know that crazed look. She used to get like this when I was growing up, and everybody would stand down. That was then. This is now! My house, God's rules!

We eat. Krista cries and tries to get me to change my mind. I'm firm because I cannot deal with her and work at the same time. I can only deal with one evil situation at a time. Then we say good night. She assures me that she will try to find a place to live in the morning. She seems well. She seems peaceful, almost like she has come to grips with what must be done.

I'm just getting into a peaceful sleep, and what to my wondering eyes should appear? Krista with a knife and coming at me fast. Okay, now I have had enough. My training as an agent kicks in, and I take her down. She is shocked. She did not know her abducted sister had it in her to fight so well. After surviving Hillbilly Hell, I learned to be a survivor. I tie her up and call the police. Guess she won't have to worry about where she is going to sleep. She is cussing like a demon as they haul her off. Good thing Officer Luke does not show up. He will have had to ask his boss what to do. Okay, that is a bit snarky, but right now I need snarky before I burst into tears.

Once Krista is gone, I try to relax and calm down so that I can finally get some sleep. I don't think sleep will come tonight. I just can't believe that Hillbilly Hell is invading my life once again. I'm going to check on buying a police dog. That is the only way I will feel safe in this place for the near future. Again, that stupid family has disrupted my peace. I know I said that already, and yes, I am talking to myself, or is it yelling at myself? Krista has got to be the last of them. No more! I cannot associate with them and have peace. They say you cannot pick your family, but in this case this family picked, rather, stole, me. Just because they chose to cancel my real life does not mean I have to put up with them in this current life.

I love my apartment and will not let the past interfere with it. My two-bedroom is decorated with old Amish-style furniture. My apartment is plain with light-blue walls and white trim. It is so cozy. I just refuse to let the past life change that. I love the Battenburg lace curtains throughout the apartment. I don't have a lot of pictures as I like it simple. I can think better that way. I do like the twinkle lights everywhere as little night lights. Someday maybe I can get a kitten if I can settle down long enough. The dog is still a better choice at this time.

I know my mind is just going and going right now. It isn't every day that you have somebody try to kill you while you are sleeping. Guess I should have locked the door. I can't sleep just wondering why Krista showed up in the first place. If she really hates me that much, you would think she would stay away. I am assuming she blames me for her family situation. Every now and again the good people have to win.

The Next Day

The rumor mill is flying. Who killed Patsy, and where is Krista? Michael is hanging around the office, and I'm tired of it. He acts like he has nothing to do. If he does not have anything to do, I will find him something to do. He always walks in when we are right in the middle of some important decision or trying to stop some kind of evil. He stops and listens then acts like he is looking at the day event board. Right! Should we test him on what he is looking at? The rumors will fly at any rate as I have my suspicions that Michael feeds the rumor mill.

Who gave him a key to the office anyway? That's right, the evil played on my need to treat people fairly, and I trusted Michael. Big mistake, big mistake. When will I learn to trust God, not some human?

Finding Evidence

I STILL NEED TO find the evidence that will stop Michael. If I can get the evidence, he most likely will leave. While Apollyon is very strong, Michael on the other hand is not. He does not want to go to jail, and I think he will run. Finding the evidence will be hard. Daniella and I both believe he is hiding evidence in the back maintenance shop. However, he keeps it so messy that we can't seem to find anything. I purchased markers so that we can begin to mark the tools and the equipment. You will only be able to see this mark with a black light.

Places to look: maintenance shop, maintenance closets, other residents' apartments, and finally we will have to look in every storage closet in the building. I also need to invest in new cameras so that I have a better view of this man and all the evil he tries to pull off. This will take some work, but Michael believes he is above the law, and he also believes that he will never be brought down. This is known as the Goliath effect, and we all know how that story ended up. When King David was a young boy, he killed Goliath with one stone to the head. I need to find that one stone that will bring this man down.

He seems to be able to move around and pull off all his evil. How does he get away with all the movement and evil? Nobody is perfect. I need to find his weakness. That could be easier said than done. Sometimes these things take so much time. I want God to smite them now so I can move on. My best friend once said, "Timing is everything." Okay, he was a music man, and that time I thought he was talking about music, because after all that was all he talked about. Come to find out he had a lot of wisdom in that music head of his. Yes, timing is important, and I will be patient. I noticed that Michael has increased his need for drugs and alcohol. If I can't take down a druggy with a beer issue, then it is time to hang it up and sit on the front porch in my rocker. Michael, here I come. It was so funny I used to tell him all the time that you should never try to hurt a child of God. It will not go well for you. After this, he will be a believer.

Praying, fasting, and walking helps as well. When I don't have the answers that I need, I like to pray, fast (well, I really don't like fasting, but it does help), and walk to clear my mind. Most of the time if I can just have some quiet time with God, I can hear what he is saying to me. If I listen, then I will be successful. Do I listen and do what he says all the time? No! And before you pass judgment on me because I hear things, don't most people?

Fasting usually will mean that I am drinking and not eating. I do have to have some sugar of some kind to keep my strength up. I like to walk. I can walk outside or inside either way it works.

Finding Evidence and Minding the Office

It is hard to do both at one time. Just today we have some man punch out a window. Of course it is doubled-paned, and that makes it a little more difficult to get through both of them, so he opens the bottom part and pushes the screen out then commences to toss out his furniture. Now I not only have to find the evidence to write this person up, I have to find somebody to replace the window, and I have to make sure Mr. Crazy Guy is stable. Really! I did not think I will be managing a home for crazy people, but here I am living the dream. And just when you think things can't get any more bizarre, one of the contractors working in the public bathroom gets stuck in the bathroom. The darn door just will not open. He looks like he has just seen a ghost. Now that will give me one more evil to address in this building. Hopefully he will come back and finish the job. In all fairness, I did tell him not to shut the door as he may not be able to get out. I have heard about the ghost, and one time I got stuck in that bathroom. I just never told anybody. Men, sometimes they just cannot listen. Here we go again going into battle praying.

Just last week we had to do inspections, and we were almost done when we came upon a younger resident that needed to clean off his stove top so that he did not accidently cause a fire if he turned the burners on. He was not going to do it, and he started to mock me. I just looked at him and calmly stated I will be back in one week to inspect again. He looked confused. "Why?" he stated. "Well," I said, "if you are not going to clean off the stove while I'm here, I will come back every seven days until you have it done. Then every seven days for one month to be sure you keep it that way." He turned and started to clean the stove off. I guess he was not happy about our visiting him on numerous occasions. And his entire freezer was full of clothes and shoes.

And let's not forget the carpet killer. That was a real piece of work. People, the killing must stop! The inspections must happen. It is just that way. Then we must look at the crazy people that live here. Growing up in Hillbilly Hell, we had a mental institution that was across the field from us, and I never thought too much about it. I am thinking about it now! These poor people need more help than I can give.

Daniella and I are so tired at the end of the day. We just go home and fall asleep. I must confess this assignment is a bit challenging because of all the crazy people. I know you are probably thinking like I am that I should be used to the crazies, but do you ever really get used to them? And they can make you tired.

My Day Off

I GET ONE COMP day a month. I created this day off because I am at work early and leave late every day. This is usually my hair day, and the nice residents call it my holy day because I must go and get my hair done. This month is no exception. I am getting my hair done no matter what. If they only knew I don't always get this time for me.

I tell Daniella that she is not to bother me unless the place is burning to the ground. I need at least one day of quiet.

On my chosen day off, I get my hair done, get coffee, and shop for a new outfit. Then I go home to rest. The next day will be long. I'm sure there will be a lot to follow up on.

The next day.

New hairstyle, check!

New outfit, check!

Coffee, lots of coffee, check!

Prayer, check!

Now I am ready to take on the fight! I feel like I fight these residents every single day. Why can't they see I have a job to do and that is all I want to do? If they would let me, I could have this place up and running in no time. They just see it as an us-against-them thing. Is that even a thing?

As I drive onto the property, I see that somebody tossed trash everywhere and then they tossed an entire watermelon in the middle of the field. Nice! I wonder which one of the delinquents did that and thought it was a great idea? Well, we will look at the camera and see who the genius was.

Next, I make it into the front door, and a line of people are waiting to talk to me. I feel like I have been at work for six hours, and I really have only been here for about an hour. When is my next day off? Oh, no, you don't! I'm not going to let this gang stop me from enjoying my life. I love my job! I love my job! Right?

I open the window, and first up to the window is April. She had some guy's car towed, which she had no business doing, and now we will have to pay him back. She is out of control. Sarah is next. She states that bugs are eating through her icebox and her food is going bad. She states that she has bugs all over her bed and they are attacking her. We need to kill them or something. God, please don't let me roll my eyes, but we did address this last week after she called my boss and threaten to call the news people.

Finally, Daniella shows up with more coffee! God bless her! Now she can help sort out this craziness.

"Okay, first, Sarah, you don't have bugs eating through the freezer and eating all of your food. It just seems like it because your sister is trying to kill you with the drugs she is giving you." Of course, I can't say that! I open my mouth to talk to Sarah. "Sarah, we will come up to the apartment and see what we can do. Give us a couple of hours, okay?" She finally agrees. She states that she will go out and eat at a Sonic since there are no bugs at Sonic. Good to know in case I stop for supper.

Daniella takes the next one! It is Susan. She states that her AC is not working, and if she turns it on, all it does is run. Daniella tries to explain to her that it is 105 degrees outside, and yes, it will run if she wants to stay cool. Susan does not understand this, and she blames it on the contractor that changed her filter. I can see it is going to be one of those days. Wait, hasn't it been one of those months.

The Tweeker

Poor guy did not know what hit him. He seemed so nice when I first showed up, but then as days went by, one of the gang members gave him some meth, and he was hooked. Now he is just terrorizing the people in the building. I suggest to Daniela that we look on the cameras to see if there is anything happening that would hurt the residents since they are upset with him. After we take care of the complainers at the window, we take our coffee into the camera room. We watch the tweeker run around like a nut and put a melon in the field. Okay, what is up with the melon in the field? He then goes around the building waving his arms and hands shouting it is going to blow. Now that is a twist on summer watermelon.

Nothing stands out, and we continue with our search as we watch the footage. Usually as we watch the cameras, we find all kinds of rule breakers. As we suspected, here is a group of the gang members following one of the residents into the building. They taunt her until she begins to cry. I get so upset with the gang and with the people who will not report them. I'm sure they are afraid for their life. Okay, that does it! Now it is time to begin to minimize every member of the gang. They will leave or they will get out of the way. Either way works!

The tweeker is just hurting himself now. Time to move on to something else. I rise to go into my office so that I can do some paperwork. There is that word again, *paperwork*, so much to do, so little time. As I stand to walk into my office, a gunshot goes off. I'm stunned to hear the gun go off, then I'm stunned to find out that I'm hit. There is red-hot blood running down my nice new shirt. I think this crosses some kind of red line in the sand. Not only is this painful, but I must buy a new shirt, and I liked this shirt.

Daniella looks like she is going to faint. I try to smile and suggest she call 911.

Hospital Scene

I DO NOT LIKE doctors, and hospitals are the worst. I always feel like they are dirty, and I can see evil at every corner. Great, one of the gang members followed me here. What, are they going to try and finish the job? Finally, my name is called. The staff tells me it will only be a moment longer. There are a lot of stabbings and shootings today. Well, now if that doesn't beat all, I'm not the only one with a bullet hole in me.

I ask them if I can just walk around a little until they get me into a room and a bed. They did not see anything wrong with that. I walk down one hall, and there are a lot of lights on and TVs on, but nobody is home. I take a moment to look around, then I get out of there. It appears as if I am the only human there at the time. I go back the way I came and sit in the waiting room. This is what I hate about emergency rooms, the motto seems to always be hurry and wait.

While I'm sitting there, I start to look back at what happened. Does somebody really hate me that bad they would try and shoot me?

Daniella and I need to have better security. I'm thinking stunned guns and a dog. I want a police dog. Then we need to start some kind of camera watch with documentation so that we can figure out who is the leader of this gang and who wants me dead. After I get my wound taken care of, I call Daniella to see if she can come get me, and then we need to stop and get a new shirt for me. She tells me she is on her way.

Once she picks me up, and we are in the car I talk over security ideas. She liked them, so we just needed to put them in motion. We talk and try to figure out who was shooting at us. The cameras need to be updated and more of them. That is the first step, after I get a new shirt, of course. We looked at the cameras we have now, and we could not see the shooter. Next, we need to find out where I can buy a police dog. Daniella is working on the stunned guns for us.

The next day is Friday, and I must take off to rest so my arm will heal. Daniella assures me she will be fine. A long weekend to rest is probably what I need.

Friday, I sleep until noon. I haven't done that in a while. I remember growing up with Jack and Lucy, sometimes we would all sleep until noon. Now that I look back on my past life growing up with Jack and Lucy, the great parents they tried to be, were probably giving me drugs to make me sleep.

Once I am awake, I realize that I need to do something to dial back the stress. You guessed it, new shoes, new purse, and chocolate. Then I will stop for supper and come home to watch one of my favorite movies about an Amish girl and her choice of men. As I shop, I can feel the tension leave. I know this is not a good way to beat stress, but it sure is fun. I will not spend as much as some people do going to a shrink and taking pills. I have nothing against counselors or taking pills if that is what you need. What I need just happens to be shopping and chocolate. There is a small café that serves the best Italian food really close to my apartment. I will stop there on my way home.

I don't usually like eating alone at a restaurant, but today I will make an exception to lower my stress level. As I'm seated, I notice the most handsome man sitting across the aisle. I order my food and try not to let him see me looking at him. Too late! He catches me! He smiles, and I'm thinking, *Is he smiling at me or is there somebody standing behind me?* I smile back and then start to eat the bread that is served before the meal.

The next thing I know he is standing at my table. I try to act cool. "Cool," who even says that anymore, and why am I thinking it? He asks me if he can sit and finish his meal with me. Okay, sure, why not! We begin to talk, and I find out he is a private investigator. So I ask him if he is eating with me as part of an investigation. I am teasing, but he is not really that reassuring. Hmm, moving on. We eat and have small talk. When we are almost done eating, he asks me if he can see me again.

Well, let's see, I'm in the witness protection program, I have no idea who my parents are, and the people that raised me are human traffickers. That about covers it. I shake my head out of my fog. "Sure, it would be nice to go out again," I say. Did I just say that? As I look at the handsome guy with the beautiful blue eyes, black hair, and a smile that will melt any girl, I realize I just agreed to have a date with this guy. I try to be cool or something. I suggested, "Give me your business card and I will call you when I'm available." I try to explain that my job is very up and down. He just laughs and gives me his card.

As I head for my apartment, all I can think about is who this guy is and what I can dig up on him before I call him. To say that I have trust issues would be an understatement. I realize that he did not ask me my name and I did not ask his. This is either the most romantic thing that has happened to me or the deadliest. Only time will tell. Prince or serial killer? My mind has got to stop this. After seeing so many bad things happen to nice people, I must know more about the subject since I must be very cautious.

When I reach my little apartment, I look at the card. His name is Paul English. Well, that is a start. I can google his name and business to see if he is who he claims to be. As I begin my search, I found out he has been in business for five years and served in the military for twenty years. Not a bad beginning. Now let's see if he has a Facebook page. That will usually tell you everything you want to know about a person. I see he likes dogs, goes to church, and graduated from a local university. This all says normal. I just have one question, why did he not ask my name? Does he always pick up strange women?

I continue to look at his handsome face with the baby-blue eyes looking back at me. Could this guy be real?

The next day I call Paul and we set a date. Should we call it a date? I have not been out for so long I can't imagine what this is going to be like. Daniella thinks I should stop the worry and enjoy a night out. We will see.

I meet Paul at the Mexican restaurant in my neighborhood. I am not going to have him pick me up at the house. Then again, if he is any kind of investigator, he already knows where I live. As we get seated, we order our drinks. I'm having lemon water so that I can keep my wits about myself. Paul has a soda. We smile at each other, then we begin to chat. Paul finally tells me he is investigating the carpet killing at the complex where I work.

I did not see that coming. Is he investigating me, the killing, both, or is he just using me to get some information? It is so hard to always mistrust somebody. We talk, and I try to interrogate him so I can figure out what he is up to. Finally Paul laughs and states, "I'm not here to investigate you. I really did notice you at the restaurant for the first time."

I ease up on him a little. He can say all he wants. He is dating me and investigating the carpet killer, and I will have a wait and see attitude. After supper, we decide to go to the park and walk off the supper. It is quiet, and it is easy to talk with Paul. I sure hope I am not making a big mistake.

We both decide to call it a night because we both had to work. He asks me if he can come out and talk to some of the residents. I explain, "Sure, I will give you access, only if they want to talk with you and if you promise to share what you find. Everybody is so nervous with all the killings, I mean, deaths at the complex." Paul agrees. "See you in the morning," he says. I remind him that he should not let on like he knows me. They may not talk to him. Paul just smiles and says, "Not very well-liked, are we?" I just laugh and go home.

While at home, I get the whiteboard out. Paul goes in the center as he is the investigator. I look at the areas we talked about. One item I did not remember to ask him was who sent him to investigate. Tell me it is Officer Luke and I'm going to roll my eyes. I just know I will. It is a question I must remember to ask Paul.

Now I must dress up for work the next day. After all, I want to dress to impress! This could be fun dating an investigator, at least for now. Should he decide to get serious, I will have to share my past with him.

The Next Day

I WAKE UP EARLY. I select my black pants, blue top, and a black blazer. I add a cross necklace and a bracelet. I head out the door on my way to get my coffee.

I go to work earlier than usual. I was looking forward to seeing Paul and to start the investigation. The usual suspects are all here. What are they doing up so early? They all look just a little evil in their own special way. All except Betty Sue. She always is so cute looking for an elderly lady, and she walks slow with her cane. She just brightens everybody's day with her smile. Now they all could be like Betty Sue, this place may not be so bad.

I have a mountain of paperwork to do. I see we have ten complaint forms in our drop box. Of course, we do! Some people have nothing better to do in their life. Here is a good one. This resident is complaining because her stove was not clean enough when she moved in, even though she signed paperwork to accept the apartment the way it is. Guess I will send her a sweet little note along with paperwork to move out if she wants to.

Here is some mail from the main office. That can't be good. They will have more paperwork for me to do. And of course, we have bills to pay. A ton of bills to pay. That's okay, I'm smiling because I know Paul will be here soon. I sound like a schoolgirl. How crazy is that?

Daniella is finally here. I can fill her in on everything. One good report, nobody died last night, so maybe the killer slept all night.

Daniella wants to know how my date went with Paul. So the story begins. I tell her that dating was fun and not fun all at the same time. She thinks I'm losing it. Maybe I am, but I have such huge trust issues. If I could know that I could trust Paul, then I would be having the time of my life even in the middle of the killings.

I told Daniella how we had supper and went to look for antiques for my home. She knows how much I love old things, especially books. I can just imagine the author sitting at his or her desk when they are penning each word. I would love to be a writer seems like it is much calmer than being an investigator.

I tell her while at supper, we discussed the carpet killing and he told me that he was here to investigate the killing. I explain that while talking with Paul about the gang and the killings, if Paul turns out to not be trustworthy, I will throw him to the gang of hate that tries to rule this place. And of course, Daniella sucks in wind and says, "Victoria, you will not!" I laugh and state, "Of course not, but it was a fun thought."

Daniella and I go over the carpet-killing events. We think it was quite strange that somebody would kill an old lady, roll her up in a carpet, and throw her down the trash shoot. Not much imagination in that killing. Now we are trying to figure out who it would be. I suggest that it could be either Michael or it could be two or three residents. Motive could only be she ran out of drugs to sell and she knew too much. It is not healthy to know too much in this place. We still do not believe the leader does the actual killing, but he or she calls the shots. If I could just find out who the leader is and what the game is. Once you know what the game is, you can play to win. What's that saying? We either win or we learn. No losers here. I feel like I am in a long learning pattern.

Now to figure out if Patsy, the old lady in the carpet, had any enemies. Of course, she did, or she would not be dead, right?

Paul shows up to investigate. I pretend to not know him. We keep it very businesslike. He gets a temporary ID from the office and goes on his way. Meanwhile Daniella and I have time to go over the complaints from the drop box. This is always my favorite time of the day. Can nobody say anything nice anymore? I feel the urge to start to snicker, but I keep it to myself. Then I will sound like the staff at my last assignment. No thanks to that.

Bedbugs Again

How do we keep these things from getting into the complex? Now we have a young lady who has bedbugs extremely bad. We have a form, all agencies have a form. We explain to her that she needs to fill out the form and release the contents of her apartment to us so that we can wrap the stuff, throw it away, then we need to begin the purging of the little bugs from hell. Understand that bedbugs do not carry diseases. Therefore, the CDC does not look at them as threatening. They can drain you of your blood, which means that they are like vampires. They don't necessarily cause sickness, but they cause mental illness. Once you have them, you always feel like you are being bitten. Daniella and I have never had bedbugs. However, when we must address the issue, we start scratching.

We explain the procedure to her, and she refuses the instructions. Great, so now what? I talk things over with Daniella, and we look over our rules and regulations. We give her notice to move. She is really resisting, almost like she does not believe she can be kicked out over bedbugs. We continue to try and work with her. Then we realize she is being directed by the gang. Who is this leader that does not want this lady to stay here? It is my understanding that one of the gang members will be working with this lady to represent her in court.

During this time, she sits in the common areas scratching herself. She is making me itch just watching her. We try to get her to move on and go back to her apartment to no end, and she just sits there. What the heck are they telling her to make her act this way? We will see her in court. Does everything in this place have to be so hard? Why can't people just cooperate?

We will have Michael spray around the front door so that the little critters do not move out of that apartment into another apartment.

Daniella reminds me that Christmas is coming. Finally, some good news. We have Michael begin to decorate. He turns from light to evil so fast that it is hard to keep up with him. I don't care what Michael and the little evil gang think. Daniella and I love Christmas, and we will make this the best Christmas these people have ever seen. I could care less about their attitude. We will sing and be jolly. Even if it kills us, we will sing, and we will be happy. Maybe that was a little dramatic. I am sick of the killings, and we need some happiness.

Our theme this year is the Polar Express. We will put up a tree in the front with a train around it. We will hang bells on the tree. Hopefully everyone but the gang will be able to hear the bell. We are not going to party with these mean people, but then we remind ourselves that they are not all mean. The planning will now begin. We both like Christmas so much that the party begins to take on a life of its own. We have a train going down the wall, and we have lights everywhere.

Now for the stockings! We decide to make stockings and hang them all around the property. We put only first names on as these names could belong to anybody. It is going to be great. Next, we need to decide what kind of food to serve. We need to keep this part easy so it does not get out of control.

Daniella and I decide to buy roasted chicken, mashed potatoes, green beans, and a roll. It sounds pricey, but we both pitch in. For dessert, we better just have cookies. Daniella's family has stated they will help us with the food and gifts. Paul also wants to help us. We will have to discuss the entertainment later.

The trees are set in place in the lobby and in the community center where we will host the party. The place needs to be cleaned. It seems like nobody in this place will clean unless they are told to. We have a train for around each tree. We decided that in keeping with the Polar Express theme, we will have a hot chocolate station for the tenants of the building. Each morning I will come to work a little earlier than I usually do and set up the chocolate station. It seems like we are just starting to have some fun while work, and what to my wondering eyes should appear, the gang and another killing.

Daniella finds the body in one of the apartments. Everybody is trying to get into position, and they are trying to decide who they will take with them. They all want to move because they can no longer control the situation. I say goodbye and don't come back.

This time it looks like the body was drugged and left to pass away. Funny how death becomes a part of life with working in these circumstances. Only this time several of the usual suspects moved, and then there were five. This tenant was not nice, and she was downright hateful. I don't know if she did not feel well, or she just hated life. Either way, while her death was tragic, we will not miss her. How many more people will die before we get this worked out?

I just am a loss for words as we plan a party, and the gang plans the next victim. We call the police, and they take over from there. We contact some of the family members that show up acting like it is all our fault that their family member is dead.

It is almost the end of the day. I've never been so thankful to have a day over. Paul will be waiting for me so we can go out and eat. I want to find out what he knows, and I need to tell him about this latest killing. We are going to one of my favorite places to eat so that should help relieve some of the tension.

We are going to go out for steak tonight. I love steak and vegetables. Okay, I like a good hot dinner roll as well. The steaks are cooked to perfection. I trade the salad for more vegetables. Once we are seated, I begin to tell Paul about the day's events. I tell him about how Daniella is holding up under these trying times as well.

Poor Daniella is still having a hard time with the discovery of the body. She looks a little green. Hopefully she will not get sick. We really need to get our heads together and get this puzzle solved before there are no more tenants left and we won't have to worry about a party.

I told Paul at supper that I suggested to Daniella that we start to make a list of suspects and a list of the tenants would be easy to evict. Maybe we can eliminate some of them and maybe we can save some of them from being murdered.

It is Saturday!

Finally, a day off, and I really do not want to hear about murder, suspects, and puzzles. I decided to go to Harrah, Oklahoma, and see if I can find anything out about my parents. It just does not make sense that I cannot find them. Maybe this time I will have some luck, and this better not include murder and puzzles.

Harrah is a small town just east of Oklahoma City and west of Maud, Oklahoma. Harrah is small enough that one would think everybody knows everybody. It seems strange to me that nobody will talk about the abduction. I don't care if they all shun me. I will keep poking around until somebody has to talk. There is usually one person who will speak up.

Harrah has some good restaurants. My favorite is the BBQ. There is a little place off Main Street that has the best BBQ. That will be lunch. Paul will be upset when he finds out that I have gone out for BBQ without him. Sometimes, I just need to be alone and think. There is a little park off Main Street as well. I will get my food and eat there. It is peaceful, and I can get some direction from God. I'm not sure why I need to know where I came from. I suppose I thought if I was abducted, my parents will be happy to know I am alive and doing well.

It is obvious that people will not just talk with me unless they know me. My next idea is to attend church. Most of the time church people are friendly. Maybe if I attend church for a few weeks, somebody will know my mom and dad. I will just say I'm doing a story about the abduction that happened many years ago. Great! Now I am going to go to church and lie to church people. What is next? God, forgive me! Surely, they will feel safe talking about this if just for a story. We will see. Tomorrow is Sunday. We will begin.

I decided to walk around the little town and shop. Shopping always eases my tension. There are several cute shops, and the weather is great. The weather in Oklahoma is not always great, and taking advantage of this great day seems appropriate. I think finding new clothes to wear should help me feel better when I go to church in the morning.

Church

I WALK IN AND work to keep a low profile, but as we all know when you are the new person in church, everybody knows it. I smile and try to not feel intimidated. A nice girl came over to me and ask me if this was my first time at the Harrah First Baptist Church. I stated, "Yes, I'm just visiting." Once I was situated in the sanctuary, I began to feel less stressed.

Worship comes and goes. I am not completely relaxed, as I have not been inside of a church in a long while. I am asked to go out to eat lunch with some of the people that noticed I am new. Of course, I jump on that invitation.

Once we have our food and start to talk and eat, the questions start flying. I answer the best I can because I hate lying and I know I had a lot of questions in return.

Next, my turn to question the group.

"Has anybody at the table heard of the story about a baby being abducted from the front yard about twenty-five years ago?" I asked. Okay, that does not work well. Silence falls among the table. They are starting to look at me like I have two heads. I do not want to lie, but I feel the truth would not bring the answers that I want at this time.

Finally, one elderly lady states, "That was a terrible thing that happened. It was my neighbor's child that was taken." She is searching her memory for the facts of that terrible event. As she thinks, she begins her story. The story is interrupted with a call to go home. Whomever she is riding with wants to go and go now. I ask her if I can come by and talk with her some more. She is so kind and states, "Of course you can."

She leaves, and I never got her name or phone number. Now I will have to visit church one more time to see if I can talk with her. I'm just trying to figure out why that question made the table go dark for a moment. Next visit may provide more answers.

Monday Back to Work

Why does it seem like Monday is the hardest day to get started? Once I am at work, I'm okay. I just know that Monday usually brings negative complaints after negative complaints. I try to look at the positive. At least I know what is happening because they complain about everything.

Daniella and I decide to work on some Christmas stuff, and maybe that will make the day a little brighter. We need to finish the rest of the decorations and plan the party. I think being a party planner would have been more fun than hunting down a murderer, but here I am living the fun life trying to catch a murderer while trying to find out about my mother and father.

We decide to have a chocolate bar, everybody loves chocolate, and some finger foods to make it simple. Of course, we will have to find a Santa. Apparently everybody loves Santa as well.

The phone begins to ring. I don't pay much attention to it until I find out it is Paul. "Hi, Paul," I say.

Paul is a little excited. He goes on to say, "I found out some information on your little gang."

Now he has my attention. "Anything you can tell me over the phone, or would you rather meet in person?" I ask.

Paul states, "We better meet for lunch as you never know who is listening in." I agree to meet at the diner down the street from my office.

Maud, Oklahoma, is not very large, so the eating selections are not that awesome. The diner is a good and safe choice. Maud has one school and one apartment complex. Who would ever imagine that in such a small town, we will have so much murder and other crime? At least it is close to Harrah, Oklahoma, and I can easily try to find my mother.

Once we are seated, I listen to what Paul has to say. Paul begins, "A couple of your little gang members have been in prison, and a couple are suspected of killing people they were taking care of as caregivers. The ones you want to look out for, or by that I mean don't turn your back on them, are April, Donna, and Crow. All three have been in a mental hospital."

My mouth is just gaping open at this point. I ask Paul, "How did you find this information out?" He states that he cannot tell me that and it is better that I did not know anyway.

I am thinking and then I come up with a plan. I will try to have these three evicted. I know that April has been seen on camera stealing from other people in the building. Donna will be a little harder to find something on. However, it will not but impossible. Crow, who knows, I guess I will begin to lock the place down and create tighter rules. This may draw him out. "What do you think?" I ask Paul.

Paul is not thrilled with my plan. However, he does understand my need to be on the offense and not the defense.

"Now can we talk about something more pleasant, like our next date?" Paul asks. Sure, you deserve some fun after finding out that information. We decide to go to some of the parks after our dinner to see the Christmas lights that are on display. Paul, I'm finding out, loves Christmas as much as I do. I suggested we do this on a Saturday so that I can get some Christmas shopping done before we eat dinner. Paul agrees.

I don't have a lot of people to buy for, but I do love shopping. This will prove to be a great way to get into the Christmas spirit.

I tell Paul that Daniella and I are still trying to work out the details of the Christmas party. I'm sure that most of the innocent residents will love the party and the gang members will just complain. Paul states, "I would love to help in any way I can. Before I had this gig, I was a music teacher. I can lead some Christmas music if you like."

"I think we will have a cakewalk. That is always a favorite. We will supply dinner. However, presents will be in short supply since this is our first year. We hope to have some sponsors next year. Maybe we can have like an angel tree of sorts," I tell Paul.

Paul agrees, and we go on with our plans to meet on Saturday for shopping, dinner, and some light seeing before we come home. It is so nice to have something positive to think about before we must face a killer Monday. The Monday might be a killer in more ways than one.

Monday-Morning Happiness

It is Christmastime. Daniella and I start the decorating process. We ask maintenance to help us since we know the residents are not interested. They have been mistreated and threatened by this gang for so long it is going to take some time to bring life and fun back into this apartment complex. We decorate the outside and we decorate the lobby so that when you walk into the building, you can see nice decorations that just might put a smile on somebody's face.

Today we have a new resident leasing in. Her name is Jenni-Beth. That is unusual, and hopefully she is not messed up for life by that name. Who would take the time to name a child such a peculiar name? She seems pleasant enough. We know from experience that when they are signing a lease, they are always putting their best foot forward.

Jenni-Beth asks a few questions, and we begin to worry this was not a good idea. She wants to know who is in charge, and if she has any complaints, who does she address them to? Daniella and I just look at each other after she leaves and shake our heads. I suggest that we add a question to the lease. "How did you hear about us? We would like to thank the person that sent you to us." Daniella agrees. We can try to stop the influx of gang member associations this way.

So much evil, so little time!

Jenni-Beth finishes the lease in process, and the next day she begins to terrorize us. I did not see that coming. She begins with complaining about the trash rooms. I'm a little confused about the complaint until she continues to talk, and I figure out she does not want to put her stuff in a trash bag and take it to the trash can. I try to explain to her that we told her the rules while she was signing her lease and before she moved in. I reminded her that she wanted to live in the apartment complex anyway.

Who chooses to live in Maud, Oklahoma, unless you have a reason to be here?

Maud, Oklahoma, only has 863 people in it, and now it has 864 with our dear Jenni-Beth moving in. Most of the people here do not earn more than $60,000 a year, so what is Jenni-Beth's story? She does not work, so where does her income come from? She stated she had Social Security. Something tells me that she has other income. Daniella and I will have to keep an eye on her.

Then again, maybe she does have a reason to be here. Something just makes me believe that she is a friend of the gang that terrorizes this place. Hopefully her stay with us will be short-lived if she is going to make it her mission to threaten the office daily.

Daniella and I continue to decorate, and we stick to the plan to remove the evil out of here and bring life back into this place. Nobody should have to be scared in the home they live in.

Paul enters the front lobby admiring all our decorations. He asks to talk with me in the office. "Of course!" I reply. We go into the office and close the door while Daniella continues to decorate.

Paul tells me there is a lead on the carpet killer. Whoever did the killing did not have to be strong as the victim died of poisoning and she was wrapped in a carpet and, well, you know the rest. Yes, she was dumped down the trash chute. Who would do such a thing to an old woman and why? Then again, if we cannot find the answer to this question, we soon have another murder. I can just feel it in my bones.

Michael is beginning to act very irrational. It is my guess that he was close to the victim. He either gave her sex or stole her drugs. Or he gave her sex in exchange for the drugs.

I give Paul the gang member's name that I knew of. I also tell him about several little old ladies I am concerned about as they will not be able to defend themselves if they are attacked. Betty Sue is the frail one of the group. She is short, about four feet tall with gray hair, and walks with a cane. She always has a smile on her face. I really think she is so kind that the gang can kill her off without any problems.

Paul listens as I give the information that I have. I still believe that Crow is behind all the murders. Paul listens then adds, "What about Michael? Could he be in on the murders with one of the gang members?" We will begin to pay more attention to the gang members and their interactions with Michael. If we can eliminate them one by one, then we would be able to figure out who the leader is. These murders must stop. Maud does not have that many citizens to begin with, so they cannot afford to lose more.

Jenni-Beth is back for the second or is it third time today. Now she is complaining that we do not have hot coffee in the community center. Really! Now I'm supposedly here to be their coffee maker as well. Not going to happen, at least not right now. Can you just imagine me making coffee in the morning, then I go to my office, and Crow or another gang member decides to poison the coffee? Then I would go to jail for the act. That is not happening. I try to explain to her that we do not have that service currently. She comes unhinged. Is she here to bully me and Daniella on a daily, no, wait, make that hourly, basis? When will she give up? Maybe she will find another apartment complex that has coffee services and she will move, right? If only!

Paul wants to know if I want to go to dinner with him tonight. I state I would love to. We agree to meet at 6:00 p.m. Since I'm on duty tonight, we agree to meet at the restaurant in case I must leave early. We are meeting in a town close to Maud so we can talk. We are going to one of our favorite places to eat. It is a steak house with the best vegetables and rolls I've ever tasted. Paul leaves.

I fill Daniella in on our conversation. She also thinks that it is Crow is the problem and we must keep an eye on the elderly that live at the complex. I feel like they are not safe.

We are about to close the office for the day, and what do we see? Jenni-Beth and Crow sitting in the community center talking. I wish I have cameras with audio down there. Not that it would matter if we have all the security in the world, the two of them together are trouble. Where did this Jenni-Beth come from?

December 18

We only have a few days left until Christmas. The Christmas decorations look great, and we all seem to be working together. We begin to plan our Christmas dinner. The dinner will include food, music, and games. We will have door prizes as well. I've learned from my experience with my past assignments, people love to win something, anything. We will give away money in different denominations. We all love getting money. The cakewalk speaks for itself. Store-bought cakes only so there is no poisoning going on.

The chime at the window rings. It is Susie! She states she has bedbugs. Our company will handle the bedbug situation. However, Susie will have to cooperate. I explain to her what we need for her to do and what she needs to do. She agrees. On her way back to her apartment, Crow approaches her. "Susie, you do not need to trash any of your stuff, she cannot make you. And she will still have to treat you for bedbugs. Trust me on this."

We have pest control come in, and they tell us that Susie has not cooperated and that they sprayed the best that they could under the circumstances. I call Susie into the office, and she explains about the conversation with Crow. I tell her that if she does not follow the procedure by twelve noon on the nineteenth of December, we will evict her as she is dragging bedbugs all through the building. She laughs and goes on her way. I knew she is not going to do what was expected of her, so I start the eviction paperwork for her to issue at 1:00 p.m. on the nineteenth.

We are still trying to decide if we should evoke Santa to be at our party. I would love to, but Daniella reminds me he may not be safe. We may have to skip Santa for this first party until I see if there is any criminal activity.

We continue with our plans for food, music, and games for the party. We decided to have them sign up so we know how much food we need and how many door prizes we need so that everyone is served.

Time to go home and prepare for my dinner date with Paul. I wonder if he will want to stay with me when he finds out who I really am. I will worry about that later. I just pray that I can come out of hiding soon.

I go home, then I change into my nicer clothes and go to the restaurant. Paul is waiting for me, and we go to our table. I order my favorite steak and vegetables. We begin to talk about all that has happened today and where we should go next. I suggested that if I put pressure on Michael, I do believe he will cave. He is not that strong. I will try to get him to hand over some of the gang and their activities. Maybe we can catch them in the act of killing.

Paul agrees, and then we begin to eat and talk about our next adventure.

Daniella texts me to let me know somebody tried to break into the office and that she would go there and secure it. We will be able to add to the security in the morning. I told her I thought that was a good choice.

I repeat to Paul what happened.

Daniella arrives at the office, and she is horrified that somebody is able to break in go through all the files and take down the cameras. She is trying to secure everything until morning, and she feels a knife at her throat. A husky sounding voice whispers in her ear. "Tell that new manager to back off or she is going to lose her sidekick, meaning you." The stranger cut Daniella's throat just enough to draw blood. He backs out of the office, and of course, nobody sees anything. The darn cameras do not always work.

Daniella calls the police to report the break-in and the attack on her. Once the police arrive, they realize this was not an idle threat, and they suggest we do not come here alone until they find out who is up to this kind of threat.

Daniella calls me to give me an update. I tell her to make sure she walks out with the police and tomorrow we will have the security system updated. I tell her I am so sorry for what she has to go through, and we will make some changes. She assures me it is okay and they she would be back at work in the morning.

December 19

I arrive at work at 7:00 a.m. so I can begin the cleanup and I can call around to find somebody to update our cameras. As I start the clean, I realize that there are no files missing, but I do notice some blood from where they stabbed Daniella. It is almost 8:00 a.m., so I better get ready for the day. I must check on Susie, or bedbug lady. If she has not complied, she must leave.

As I prepare to open for the day, I see Susie, and she is telling me she is ready and that she has done as much prep work as she can. I tell her that if she is not ready, we are going to have to take her to court to evict her. She does not seem to care. She does not understand that you cannot give bedbugs to the entire building. First, that would cost a lot of money to exterminate the little critters, and second, I will not want to stay here. Bedbugs are just horrible. After I talk with her and explain the situation, I watch to see where she goes. I think she will run right to Crow's apartment, and she does. He is just messing with her as he believes if I evict her, then I will be the one in trouble. Then again it would be just like Crow to want the entire building covered in bedbugs.

That does it, I'm calling the camera company right now. I need a total update on the cameras. Then I need to make sure our locks are secure. Daniella is here now, and I want to talk with her to make sure she is doing okay. She assures me that she is fine and that her neck is not hurt all that badly. She is explaining that it is just a scratch, enough to draw blood. The intruder is trying to scare us off. I tell her that we will be more cautious from now on. She agrees.

Michael comes to the office. Of course he is trying to find out what happened so that he can report back to the gang. At this point, I don't even want to feed him any kind of information, true or not. I really don't think I have the energy to give out misinformation right now. He, of course, is angry because we will not let him in, and we will not give him any information. Just once could he start working and stop the shenanigans. There must come a point when we have enough evidence to rid ourselves of this man. Too bad too because he really is a good maintenance person. We will keep watching him.

The Bullying Has Become Personal

Ever since we leased to Jenni-Beth, we have had trouble. She seems to want to bully the office. This is confusing because up until now, most of the bullying has come from residents to residents. For some reason unknown to us, Jenni-Beth hates the office staff. She appears to have only one friend here in the building, Crow. Did Jenni decide to break into the office? And if she did, will she be strong enough to overcome Daniella? Daniella and I brainstorm this for a while. I guess anything is possible. Why is it so personal?

I have no idea where this bully and the bullying would have come from. Do adults need to have a reason to bully, or do they just make things up as they go? As we know that if you are being bullied, the bully either sees you as a threat or just plain hates you. Maybe you hurt them or somebody they are close to and that is why they bully you? I only know Jenni-Beth from this assignment. The gang has probably figured out by now that she is a little off and they can use her to get to the office. Great, just one more threat to worry about. Paul is not getting anywhere with the carpet killing. The killer has just gotten away with murder.

Since Krista is out of the picture, I will go home and work the wipe board. Surely if I write it out, pray, and then study the situation, there must be an answer. People don't just wake up and decide to hate a person without a reason. Usually, the bully has a reason for the targeted bullying. It could be they want power over that person, or they just want to see that person feel hurt and confused. No matter what the reason, it is evil and in the case of this gang, it has led to murder.

It Is Sunday

I DECIDE TO GET up early and go to Harrah for church. I want to see if I can find out any more information about my birth family. Church starts at 11:00 a.m., so I need to get a move on. Once in church, I tried to find the nice lady that befriended me the last time I was here. She did not seem to mind talking about the abduction.

We sing for a while, and the pastor gives his sermon. Once church is over, I look around to find my friend, and she is nowhere to be found. I ask some of the people that I remember from the last time I was here. We all went to lunch together, so I ask them if they know where she is. They look surprised that I do not know that she died. I gasp at the thought. "How did she die?" I ask.

The answer is not what I expected. "She died after she talked with you and got so upset that you tried to find out about her daughter. It was not a good time in her life, and the memories of that time were horrific."

Now I am quite stunned, but I am wondering how things between this woman, who apparently was my grandmother, and her daughter could have been as horrific as growing up in Hillbilly Hell with Jack and Lucy? I just stare at the group and walk away. Now how would I find out what happened on the day Jack and Lucy abducted me?

I walk to my car and go home. I can't even think about this anymore. I was so close to the truth, and I had lunch with my grandmother. Why did I not tell her why I was asking all the questions? Maybe she would have embraced me. Maybe not, but I will never know. I need a vacation! I need chocolate! I need a new outfit! I sound a little needy right now. I feel needy. My very own grandmother, and she never knew her grandbaby was alive.

I call Paul on the way home. It is nice to talk to a friendly person. I know Daniella would talk me through this, but she is so busy with her family right now. I hate to bother her, and Paul and I have become better friends since we first dated.

Monday

Michael must go!

We begin to watch Michael more closely. Once we do this and track him, we can put together a case against him. This is not hard, just time-consuming. We follow him to old single women's apartments after hours. Then we catch him taking things out of the shop and loading them into a truck. I guess resale is a good market these days. The straw the does him in is when he breaks into the office and threatens me. He is expecting me to be at work early, and when he sees me in my office, he begins to threaten me. This is a strange twist of events, even for Michael. I think I surprised him because I am no longer afraid of him and the evil inside of him. It is quite interesting seeing him for one moment morph from human to evil spirit. That is a heart-stopper for a split second. His eyes turn all yellow, and for one moment he looks not so human. I still show no fear. However, I do get just a little emotional. I start screaming because I am not sure how he got into my office.

That is when I tell him he is going to be fired and that he can leave if he does not come clean with the events happening on this property. On his way out of the office, he takes a talon and scrapes it across the wall just as a reminder he is there.

I tell him not to come back in my office again. He threatens me again and tells me to watch my back. Like that is news! Does he really believe that I do not know he and his little gang are after me? One down, okay, he is not gone, but he will give me the answers I need. He is not that smart. Now I have only several gang members to go.

I want to fire him so badly, but I remembered that one saying, *"Keep your friends close and your enemies closer."* Michael will remain for now.

I start by limiting where they can congregate. No loitering in the lobby near the office, where we conduct business. No loitering on the front porch, where visitors would enter. This really makes them hate me. Good, now they will make a mistake. Hate is a funny emotion if it is not kept in check all the time. The person with the hateful spirit will eventually make a big mistake. I have never seen more hate than this gang has for the office and the staff. I'm almost afraid I will die next due to the rage that is pouring out of them.

Crow must go! I think if I can get him out of here, some of the gang members' power will be gone. I still think he is the head of this mess.

Little Betty Sue stops by the office to say, "Hi." She is too cute, and somebody needs to protect her. She is always stopping by the office and checking in with us. I can only guess she is lonely. I like talking with her.

It is almost time for Daniella and me to go home. We must straighten the office up and make sure all paperwork in behind locked doors. Then we set the cameras. I am a little tired. Playing head games can be tiring. I know we will feel better after a long night's sleep.

Tuesday

When we start the day at the office, we must spend all day planning the rest of the Christmas party. The party is tomorrow, and we want to have as much fun as we can make it for the non-evil people here. We must pick up the food and prepare the gifts. Finally, we must go over the plan with Santa so he can hand out the gifts. We talk to Santa, and he does not think it will be dangerous handing out Christmas gifts. We will have a DJ for music and a cakewalk that seems to be everybody's request. That is funny since most of them look sickly and don't need more sugar. A cakewalk it is, with all the fun cakes we can find.

Now we go to the center to decorate. This is where I shine. I like to decorate, and the more lights the better. We put a tree in the center for the Christmas real feel. Here comes Crow. All he can do is scowl, which is better than snickering. I really got tired of snickering at my last assignment. I just smile. I think that makes him madder. One of the funniest sayings I've ever heard was, "Having a positive attitude may not cure all of your problems, but it will annoy enough people to make it worth the effort" (Herm Albright). That is the goal, to make the gang all upset, and then they will do something stupid.

The stage is set, the music is in place, and the food can be picked up in the morning. I think I will lock this place down so that the evil gang can't destroy it before morning. I'm excited. Nothing like a party to help you get over the killing all around us. It will be fun to see all the smiling and not so smiling faces.

Daniella is ready to leave, and so am I. I'm sure there was some paperwork I should have gotten done, but it is Christmas, and even Santa's elves get to have some fun.

Crow makes his last mistake.

Crow is so upset at the Christmas party that he decides to threaten me and Daniella. Big mistake. He is now going to have to leave. At least, the company that owns this building does not take kindly to the staff being threatened. Two down and several more to go.

The party is going well. The food is great. the music is so much fun. Daniella and I were eating and dancing with the residents. The chocolate fountain was a huge hit. I liked the chocolate fountain as well. Okay, I like chocolate, fountain or not. I like shopping as well. These are my therapy sessions. The way I look at it, I can pay some-body else to listen to my issues or I can talk to God, eat chocolate, and shop. I really need to watch that last one, shopping. That can be quite costly. So far this has worked for me, and I don't have to worry about bringing in yet another person to talk with.

We hand out gifts that Daniella and I purchase over the last week or two. The gifts are a hit. The residents have fun opening the gifts, taking selfies with Santa, and eating more food. I have never seen so much food. I have to say that Daniella and I really put on a good show.

As I turn on the dance floor and start toward the kitchen, there is Crow. Crow looks at me and says, "You better watch your back, because I am coming for you." Wow, have I just heard a threat come from his mouth? I am in so much shock my mouth was gaping open. Daniella notices and decides to come over to see what happened. Then Crow looks at Daniella and states, "You better watch your back as well." He goes on with his threat. "I know where you all live, and I will send somebody to stop the torture you are placing on these people."

Now Daniella is standing with her mouth open as well. I turn and call the police. The police come and take our statements. Basically, we can give a statement that turns into a paper trail. Unless somebody kills you, it really does not count. Crow then proceeds to go to his apartment and start smoking. That does it, I've had enough of this overgrown bully. I type the paperwork for him to leave or be evicted. I feel sure he will not leave on his own. I will have to toss him out. Which usually means court, and that usually means money. Why can't people who are so evil just leave when they have been defeated? I guess that is another story.

The party is over. All the nice residents had a great time, and that makes it all worth it. Now I must go to the office and start writing Crow up.

Crow continues his rampage until the end. Susie turns out to be one of his victims. He advises her not to do anything about the bedbugs, and she listens to him. What kind of mindless person will listen to somebody like Crow. I just know he is the head of all this trouble.

The main office calls and wants me to write several new policies for bullying, attacking the office, and a few other policies. As it turns out you must have a policy to cover everything, or somebody is going to take you to court over whatever they deem unfair.

Christmas Break

Apparently even the little people like me and Daniella get to have some time off for Christmas. This comes at just the right time. I need some downtime to work on the board at home. Daniella is just as excited as I am. She looks worn out. Sometimes we need to crash and burn, which means we need chocolate and sleep usually in that order. When I crash and burn, I can sleep for three days. Once I do this, watch out because I am back on my game. A good way to lose a battle, any battle, is to be stressed, not eat chocolate, and not get enough sleep. Merry Christmas to us. I will work on the policies later. Daniella agrees. She can't go another day without a break. We all need to get recharged.

December 26

Daniella comes to work before I can. I have a huge headache and am moving a little on the slow side. She does her normal walk through the apartments, and what does she discover, one of our little gang members has been smoking weed, and when she opens the door, it is clear she breaks in on a deal going down as well. She calls the police, and they come out right away. She stands her ground and never leaves the apartment until the police comes. They arrest several of the gang members. I can only guess these are the not-so-smart members.

Donna, Sarah, and Jenni-Beth are all arrested. Donna is screaming that we will pay for this and that we better watch our backs. What's new, Crow already informed us of the situation and that they are all coming for us. Sure! We will see! But just in case, we will step up security in the building and at our homes for a while. Jenni-Beth was the most vocal. Why does that lady hate us so much? She acts like she has a vendetta against Daniela and me. Someday she is going to explode if she does not tone down some of that anger.

Once the news is out that they are arrested, the other gang members are trying to make their way to the door as well. It is taking them a little longer since they are not going to jail. They need to find a new roof over their heads.

Later that day we hear that Jenni-Beth is killed while in jail. She apparently has an attitude with one of the inmates and they start a fight that Jenni-Beth can't finish. The other inmate is stronger and filled with more hate than Jenni-Beth, which is surprising to me. Jenni-Beth seems to be full of a lot of hate, but then again that is probably just directed toward me and Daniella. To this day I will never understand why she was full of such rage. She was! That was her downfall. As information begin to leak, the other gang members try to get out as fast as they can.

Time to Go Home
for the Night

It is finally 5:00 p.m., and we are exhausted. Where does the time go? It is not all bad. It is just exhausting winning sometimes. I will do all the paperwork in the morning, and we will work on a system to do welfare checks on the remaining residents. I hope Betty Sue is not to upset and that she is not scared. Bless her little heart. She is just so cute with that smile and cane she uses to support her. Betty Sue does not seem to get upset no matter what is happening around her. She is something else.

As I leave, I receive a phone call from Paul. "Paul, how are you doing?" I ask.

Paul states that he is doing great and that he wants to talk with me this weekend. I'm so tired, but I tell Paul Friday night will be great and we can go out to eat.

As the week is ending, I realize that if I am going to have any peace, I need to get my paperwork caught up.

I need to get to work early so that I can get end-of-year paperwork ready, write the policies that are needed, and get a form of rule book together for the residents. We all seem to be flying by the seat of our pants right now.

Paul agrees to pick me up at 6:00 p.m. on Friday for our date. At least I have something fun to look forward to. Paul is acting a little on the strange side. He is way too excited, and I'm not sure what for. We are eating at a restaurant that we usually eat at. Oh, never mind, I will just enjoy the excitement he has about going out.

Friday Morning

I LOVE GOING TO work at 6:00 a.m. so that I can get all my paperwork caught up. I never seem to have enough time during the day to get it all together. I thought through some of the policies that are needed in the place. I want to encourage the residents to look out for one another. I set out to create the buddy system. What is the buddy system? Thank you for asking.

The buddy system will explain to the residents that they need to get to know their neighbors. "You don't have to be best friends, just find out a few things about them and how often do they go outside of the apartment, if they will tell you this. Once we know the patterns of each other, you can call in a welfare check if we don't see that person for a while. This could save lives if someone has fallen or needs help in other ways. We can always call 911." Once this system is perfected, I run off enough copies for every resident, copies for in the lease packets, and copies for on each floor.

I then proceed to get the accounting done for the end of the year and write the rest of the policies.

Some of the policies I will write today will be more for the tenants' safety. Like don't bully, what a novel thought. Pet policy and rent policy, which will include how to take rent and what form of money we will accept. We need to include a deposit and a pet deposit. We will no longer accept cash so that we cannot be accused of stealing, like the director before me. I better add a policy about smoking and drugs. Also, one about drinking outside of their apartments. One would not think you would have to have so many rules for adults, but you do.

Writing the policies is not as bad as doing the other paperwork. How do I get stuck with these jobs that have so many pieces of paper that I am responsible for? I am extremely happy that I have Daniella as she does not seem to mind all the paperwork. She seems to have a system that gets it done. She does not let it upset her either.

It is almost 4:30 p.m. I've worked until I cannot see straight. I need to go home and prepare for my date tonight. I ask Daniella to close for me, and she agrees.

The Proposal Date

I GO HOME AND get out of my work clothes. We are going to go to Cattlemen's steak house tonight. I love steak, and this place has the best steak in the world. Paul knows how much I love eating here. I guess he is just being extra nice tonight since Daniella and I have had such a hard week. Sometimes I just want to sleep for twenty-four hours straight. However, a girl must eat, and this is the best place to eat.

We arrive at the restaurant and Paul finds a parking space not far from the door. Thank you, Lord, as I'm so hungry and tired that walking would prove to be a chore. Once in the restaurant we are seated at a nice table beside the window. I like the window so I can people watch. Not sure if I like to people watch because people are funny, or I just like to watch my back. I've never been a very trusting person after growing up in Hillbilly Hell. I've never really trusted too many people after that.

Once seated I noticed a dozen roses at our table. That's odd. I have not seen roses at any other table. Then the waitress leaves the menus and takes our drink order. Now I'm starting to think something is up when Paul is sitting across from me smiling like the cat that just ate the canary. Why do I always think it is going to be something bad? After all, how bad can it be with a dozen roses sitting at our table? I open the menu and almost fall to the floor even though I was sitting. Inside the menu and large letters is, "WILL YOU MARRY ME?"

Oh, Paul, if only I can say yes! "Paul." I look at him with tears in my eyes.

Now he is beginning to look at me with a sad and doubtful face. "Honey," he says, "I'm not trying to make you cry."

Now it is my turn. "Paul, I want more than anything to say yes. However, you have no idea who I am and what my past is like. I'm not who you think I am, and it would not be fair of me to say yes at this point in our relationship. Can we just eat and go home?"

We ate in mostly silence. It was the worst dinner I've ever had since leaving Hillbilly Hell.

Once we come home, I explain that I need some space and I need to think. He is nice enough to smile and say he will be waiting to hear from me after I have time to think.

This weekend sucks!

I just wanted a steak dinner, some conversation with my friend, and then some rest. What a production. Never in a million years did I see that coming from Paul. I know he is starting to like me, and I am falling in love with him, but I don't think we can make this work. He does not know my past and how I must live now. Would he want to live undercover on dangerous missions until the gang at the border gets over the hate that they have for me?

Weekend is over. Back to work!

I hate leaving Paul hanging, but I have no choice. I want to talk with him about my situation before I make a commitment. I'm sure he will never talk to me again. The look on his face was devastating.

Back to writing policy and checking out the latest crime in the building. As I begin to write my new policies, I receive a visit from the police. *Who died now?* I'm asking myself. Why can't these guys show up with some good news once.

I put on my smile and greet them. "What is up?" I ask them.

They proceed to ask me if I know a lady by the name of Anna Bowers. I say, "Yes!" They then tell me she was killed over the weekend, and would I have any ideas about who killed her? I ask them, "How do you know she was killed and not just died?" They state that she was stabbed and sent flying into the wall of her apartment. I agree, sounds like a killing to me. I'm so upset. Who will protect these elderly people in this complex?

I wish I can call Paul and talk this over with him. I can't call him because he will get the wrong impression. Daniella and I will just have to figure this one out on our own. "You say she was stabbed and sent flying into a wall. I would assume that this person was large and could overpower somebody like Anna?" The police agree.

Great! I will get the board out and get the list going. Poor Anna, just leased in no more than three months ago. She would never have come to this place if she knew this would be where she would meet her maker. I get the chills just thinking about it. I'm always watching my back and trying to watch the back of our elderly residents. Where did the knife go that was used on Anna? It did not just disappear.

Maybe my first policy should be no killing in this building. Okay that sounds stupid, but all the killings are just a little redundant, don't you think? What! Do they wait for the staff to go home for the weekend and then decide who the next victim will be? That just sounds crazy to me.

When Daniella arrives, I inform her of the resident that died, oh, wait, was killed. There is a difference. She looks stunned. I'm stunned. We have coffee and try to figure out who this killer is. Then I tell her that I must get some policies written and she needs to increase our security. She agrees, and we get to work.

First policy

If you see something, say something. If we have more eyes on the lookout, then we can stop the killings. The more time we are at the ready, the faster we can close in on this person. I suggest that if they fill out a paper with information about what they see, we will run with it. The police seem to be a little laid-back, but Daniella and I can pick up the pace and figure this out.

Second policy

Bullying will not be tolerated. If you are being bullied or know of somebody being bullied, then come talk to the office, and we will stop the bullying. We will evict those people who are doing the bullying. Better yet, if we can prove the bullying, then we will have them arrested. Once arrested, they will be evicted and banned. If you are afraid to tell, then use the form in the lobby to write that you are being bullied and by whom. You do not have to sign the form. It will just take a little longer to find the threat.

L.A. Ward

It is nearing our lunchtime, and after much discussion, Daniella and I decide to get lunch and eat at the office so we can discuss the murder that just took place. We decided on one of our favorites: tacos. While Daniella is on her way to get our food, I set up the whiteboard so we can talk and eat.

Whiteboard

I BEGIN TO LIST the players that we knew were gone.

June is dead, probably at the hands of April.

April moved to another apartment complex.

Donna is in jail.

Sarah is in jail.

Crow is evicted and banned.

Jenni-Beth was killed in jail.

Susie left due to bedbugs.

Anna Bowers is dead as of this weekend.

Betty Sue (bless her heart) is still walking around with her cane. Betty Sue does not seem to be upset or touched by these murders. Maybe it is because she is elderly, and everything is just great in her world. Maybe she knows enough to stay out of the line of fire.

Jane is still here, but she appears to be too elderly to have committed such a brutal crime.

Daniella is back with our food, and I'm starving.

As we eat, we look over the list.

I just can't figure out who would be strong enough to do this deed. Anna wasn't frail, or I should say she did not appear to be frail. This looks like a male would have done this. Then all of a sudden, we look at each other with horror in our eyes. "Michael," we both say at the same time. Why did I not see this coming? He probably has been killing people all along and making it look like the gang members were doing it. Or he is working with the members of this gang to kill the other residents they do not agree with.

We both decide it is time to put a stop to this ongoing killing spree. How did this slip past me and Daniella? Daniella was always warning me that I should get Michael off this property. I knew he had to go, but he was being silent as the property continued to endure killing sprees.

Paul calls.

I roll my eyes as I feel like this is just one more thing I must deal with. Sometimes I believe it will be easier to just walk away and not have any ties to others. I'm sure that is not a healthy attitude, so here goes.

"Hello, Paul, how are you?" Dumb question. How do I think he is?

He stammers a little then asks if he can come over and bring supper. I hesitate for one moment then cave. "Of course, you can come over," I say. "It has been a while." We agree on a time, then I go back to work.

How can I prove that Michael and some other person around here is doing all the killing? Most of the gang has left the building, so it only leaves Michael, and who? I really need to get a handle on this before we lose other residents. I need to be sure Betty Sue is safe. She looks so fragile, like she would break in a windstorm. There must be a way to get some of these people to talk about what is going on around here. I just need one person to talk, and others will follow.

In all this time, I completely forgot about Michael. I know he is doing underhanded deeds, but murder, that seems like it is a bit much for even Michael. As I sit here pondering my next move, I pray for some creative thoughts right about now. Michael has always preyed upon the weak, and now it is time for him to go. I need to catch him and his partner. I'm not sure I believe it is somebody in the complex.

Daniella and I decided we will take turns coming into work on a Saturday for a few hours to watch the cameras. The cameras have been updated, but they are still not top of the line, and I'm afraid that we could miss something. If we come in at different times, then the residents will not be expecting us. I would like to call the police in to help us, but they would think we are as crazy as the rest of the people who live here. Better go it alone until we have some solid evidence.

We both need a break this has been one of the hardest cases I have had to deal with in a long time. We need sleep, and we need a break from here and all the evil that is in this building right now. Daniella looks like she could sleep for a week, and I feel like I could.

I know myself well, and I am starting to detach myself from this job because I need a much-needed break. Maybe I need a Monday and Friday off so I can check in at a spa that I heard about in Sulphur, Oklahoma. Then I could come back refreshed.

I remember seeing an ad for a place in Sulphur, Oklahoma. I think it is two nights for two people for 1,300 dollars. I'm not sure if this will relax me, or would I freak out at the cost and not be able to enjoy myself? Maybe a cabin in the woods where I could work on writing my journals. Sometimes I feel like I have so much to say, and of course the entire world is waiting eagerly to read what I have to say. The sound of the trees blowing in the wind, the water running in the river, and quietness would be great.

"Victoria," Daniella says. I shake my head slightly. She asks if I was okay, and I must confess to her that I am just daydreaming about a nice getaway. Daniella just smiles and states, "Don't forget to take me with you. I need a break!" I promise her if I can find a place for just one glorious day, I will sign both of us up. Who knows, maybe we can make it one day of quiet someplace where we can be pampered.

Back to my reality.

We begin to watch Michael so that we can get as much evidence of him as possible. We log everything and start filing all complaints along with the pictures we can get off the cameras to back up the complaints. You would think that with as much activity as we have around here, there would be more complaints. People either love Michael or they fear him, and I cannot figure out which it is. He is very convincing, and the elderly women love the attention.

Home for the Day

Tonight, I have supper with Paul. Maybe he won't ask me about the marriage proposal again. If he does, then I need to decide if I will tell him about my identity or just drop this entire situation. I do love Paul. But do I want to put somebody I love in danger that I am in every day. I could be in this danger all the time, like forever. What would Paul think about all this? Will he look at me like I'm a threat?

I'm in the kitchen working on shrimp scampi, my favorite. We will have shrimp scampi, salad, and rolls. I do love to cook. I don't always get the time to do this, but when I do, I like to try out my recipes on anybody who will let me feed them.

The table is set, and the food is done. Time for Paul to come. Once Paul comes to the door, I invite him in and lead him to the dining room. He is impressed with my culinary skills. I almost think I am going to be able to get through this night without baring my soul. Then after we pray and start to eat, Paul starts to lay out his ground rules. He begins, "I love you, Victoria. I need you and want you in my life. However, this will be the last time you see me if you will not marry me. I cannot go through life pretending I don't care, and it hurts to much knowing you don't care."

Okay, I did not see that coming. My shock look must have been obvious on my face. I put my head down, then I prayed and breathed. "Paul, I do love you, but you do not know my past and how I got to this place in my life."

Paul is beginning to get a little agitated. He just looks at me and states, "If you do not want this to be the last time you see me, then you need to let me in and share all with me."

"If that is what you want, I will tell you," I said softly.

"Several years ago, twenty-nine years now to be exact, I was left at a fire station in a small town in Pennsylvania, where I was adopted out to a nice family, or at least that was what I was told. The family was one that was stable, with morals and values, or at least they thought they had morals and values. They told me they loved me like I was their own. Okay, what the heck does that mean, 'like I was their own'? They were older, and when they became too old to stay at home and take care of themselves, they decided to tell me the truth of how they came to "adopt" me. They really did not adopt me. They abducted me from my front yard. I was shocked, hurt, and sad all at the same time. Too many questions about how these seemingly nice people could abduct a baby. Jack and Lucy tried to answer all my questions, and they tried to convince me that they loved me. They did not have all of the answers I needed, and they wanted me to find answers that would give me peace. They stated they would help me in any way they could. Jack and Lucy just kept begging me for forgiveness.

"I was left wondering if my parents were grieving for me after I was gone, and for how long? What is my mom's mental state now? Did my parents have more children? Maybe I will have sisters and brothers. I wonder if they still think about me from time to time.

"While growing up, I felt like something was missing, but I never could put my finger on the problem. I did not look like my mother or father. However, they assured me that I was part of the family. Then I began to think how my mother must have suffered having her child taken. I needed to find my mother and let her know that I was alive. Where to look? Jack and Lucy would only tell me that they took me from the state of Oklahoma and that it was a small town to the east of Oklahoma City. At least that was a start. After gathering as much money as I could, I decided to divorce my abusive husband from Hillbilly Hell and go to Oklahoma.

"My Hillbilly Hell husband was very abusive. No surprise there since he was a friend of the family and was part of Jack and Lucy's business. I never knew too much about the family business. I guess I never really cared. I was tired of being abused by my husband, and when I found out about the abduction, that threw me into a tailspin. This was my chance to start a new life. I always wanted to enter law enforcement, and that was my goal.

"Jack and Lucy would ask for my forgiveness many times over before I would leave for Oklahoma. Now that I look back on it, there were many girls and boys that went through our home. I was the only one that stayed all the time, except for Jack and Lucy's natural children. I was told that the children that came and went were foster kids. I never thought much about it, and I really did not care at that time. I just had to get out of that place. Looking back on my life with Jack and Lucy, it is only by the grace of God that I made it out of that situation in good mental and physical health. Okay, maybe my mental health needs some work, but I'm not serial killer crazy. I am only able to write this account of my life because God protected me in situations that were horrific for a child."

"As a child, you don't question what your parents say, and most of the time you don't question what they do. As long as your needs are being taken care of and you are somewhat happy and the world is okay. According to Erikson's stages of life theory, the first couple of years in a child's life is critical. I can thank my real mom for helping me learn to trust and have hope since I was abducted at the age of three. The other stages of life I can only assume that Jack and Lucy had some good qualities and that influenced my life in the other stages. However, looking back on my life, I had a special connection with God that the other two children did not have. I'm positive this connection helped me survive my life's situations to bring me out of this life with Jack and Lucy stronger for having the experience. However, Hillbilly Hell will always be a part of my life, and I will have to learn to use the good and the bad and be stronger for the experience.

"Once I headed for Oklahoma, I started to work in the customer service industry so I could get my degree and go to the police force. I went to the police academy and decided from there I wanted to be a border patrol agent. I was very good at what I did, and taking down the gangs was second nature to me. I was working on cases that did not seem to challenge me. That is when I decided to start Cindy's Place. It is a place where women and their children can go to leave the gang members and be safe. Once they are safe, we find out what they want to do with their lives, and we help them achieve that."

Paul does not say a word. He is just staring at me like I was either the best storyteller in the world or he never imagined what I was going to tell him. I continue with my story.

"One day I was working to infiltrate one of the meanest and hardest gangs at the border. I did, and they all went to jail. The women and children were all taken to the safe house, and the rest is history. Except one little challenge. The gang threatened to come after me.

"I was put in the FBI witness protection program, and I am now sent in to help clean up apartment complexes where the police don't seem to have the time or resources to do the job. And that would bring us to the present day. Don't you see? I do love you, but if we married, you could be in a lot of danger. I did not want to be the reason for your life to be in danger."

Paul just sat there looking at me with relief or hurt, I'm not sure which one. For the first time ever, I could not read his face. Paul then begins to tell me his story.

Paul's Story

"My name is Levi Miller. I was born in Lancaster, Pennsylvania. I was an undercover agent with the Drug Enforcement Agency. I worked with the DEA for several years, and I was very good at what I did. My main office was in Altoona, Pennsylvania.

"Altoona is the home of chocolate, Horseshoe Curve, and drugs. Large amounts of meth was being trafficked through Altoona from other states. Because of my expertise in the underground, I was asked to help. Of course, I was not going to refuse since this is exactly what I trained for all these years.

"I entered the world of drugs and found myself in the middle of a crime family. Who knew that crime families were even a thing? Apparently in Altoona, they are. I soon found out that this family controlled the entire town. They either controlled it from the outside with the businesses they owned or from the inside with the people they owned. It was hard to tell them apart.

"As I became more familiar with the workings of this family, I was able to get a lot of information about the jobs they were doing and the drugs they sold. One of the main sources of their income was from prescription drugs. I found out that there were several doctors that would write a prescription for a patient, then the patient would be paid money to hand over the prescription to the crime family. The crime family would then take the pills and sell them on the street. This crime would leave only the doctors involved vulnerable. If the crime family trusted you, then you were not in danger of losing your medical practice. If they did not trust you, then you would either lose your medical practice or your life.

"One day there was a body found somewhere in Blair County that could only be a connection to the crime family. This body was thought to be a body of an informant and was helping the police zero in on the family. I was approached with this information and asked if

I could find out any information. Of course, I was going to try and stop this crazy family from killing anymore citizens.

"I was moving up in the family, and they began to trust me more and more. Once I began to be trusted more and more, I found out it was not only doctors on the payroll but police as well. Once I learned this, it was hard for me to trust anybody. At this time, I communicated with my handler and with God. God was the only one I trusted. The more time I spent with God, the more he would show me what was going to happen so I could always be ahead of the game.

"God became my mentor and friend, and that is why I felt a connection to you. I am only believing that you are a believer and that is why we felt the connection. Was I wrong?" Paul finally asked Victoria.

"No, you were not wrong in assuming that I am a believer and that I too have a connection to God," stated Victoria.

Paul continued with his story. "Everybody believes that Altoona is a sleepy little town and that crime is under control. The truth of this is the crime is under control of the crime families.

"I was sitting in a meeting with the family listening to the next big thing. Once I had as much information as I could stand or that I needed, I found a way to excuse myself and put in for a small vacation. I went to my handler and told her every piece of evidence that I had. I then requested to be in on the raid if not in the middle of it at least from afar. She agreed, and after the raid we had several people in custody. It was then that I found out the family was looking for me.

"My handler thanked me for a job well done and then suggested I go into the witness protection program. That is how Levi Miller became Paul English. To this day, I look over my shoulder. I've been blessed thus far. So you see, my dear Victoria, you and I are not so different. I did not grow up in Hillbilly Hell, but the rest of the story is so much the same."

"How can we make this work?" Victoria says out loud.

After they both ponder the question, they decide being together will be an asset and not harmful. She so wishes she can trust Paul. She trusts God, but she has a difficult time with humans. Probably from all the destruction and hate she sees around her. Victoria has a hard time believing one human could love another enough to have each other's back.

"Okay, I mean yes!" Victoria stammers.

Paul looks at her. "Yes, to what?" he states.

"I will marry you and be your wife," Victoria states in a faster-than-usual manner. She wants to be sure she does not change her mind and run.

Paul laughs so hard that his eyes are watering. He then pulls the large diamond ring and places the ring on her finger. It is beautiful. They only have to figure out where they will get married, whom they will invite that they trust. What names they will take, being the undercover people they are. How funny, most couples take the man's name, even if it is hyphenated. Not Victoria and Paul. They have to get this maniac caught, then they can choose a name. Then they can figure everything out.

Victoria goes on to give Paul details of the gang that she has so far. Once they are done talking, they decide that until this case is done, they should keep their engagement a secret except from Daniella. This will keep them safe from the gang for now.

*****

It is going to be hard not to talk about a wedding and all that would entail. There are so many things to consider. I will like to be able to find my birth mother and if she is still alive invite her to the wedding. I'm leaning toward a simple country wedding in a chapel. After all, Paul and I do not have that many friends. We also want to keep the event low-key so we don't invite any unwanted guests This wedding will be an event my heart will never forget. No matter the size, I will be marrying for love this time and not under the evil eyes of Jack and Lucy.

I have always dreamed of a white dress with lace and a lot of pearls. The dress would come to my ankles, and I would wear ankle boots. I will have a cowgirl hat. Paul can dress in jeans and a sports coat. Well, we will see.

For now, I need to crack this case. Stay alive. People are going to have to stop killing. I am beginning to take this all personally.

The Next Day

The next day Daniella and I decide to continue our watch on Michael. We decide that when people are narcissistic like Michael, he will make a mistake. We just need to catch him. It takes most of the day to track him and to figure out who his new contacts are. We finally figure out that it is not just one contact but many in the building. We look at each contact and try to find out what their backgrounds are. A clue is setting in front of our eyes. We just can't seem to get it. While we are deciding which contact to follow up on, Paul comes for lunch, and we run all the information we have passed him. We all go to the wipe board. Whomever is helping Michael, they are like a ghost. This just does not make any sense. We eat and decide to watch the cameras for a while longer. Paul decided he will blend in with the other residents for a while and try to fish out any more details.

While he is gone, our precious little Betty Sue comes by. She still looks so frail. She is smiling and asking how we are all doing. I state, "Why, Betty Sue, it is so good to see you, and we are all doing fine today." I'm not really sure she understands anything I say because she just smiles and shakes her head. Then she asks, "Can I get you all anything? You work so hard and look like you could use a break." I just shake my head now, and she moves on. I can only assume that she gets lonely. Michael better not find out that she is lonely or he will try to get close to her. She won't know what hit her if the evil one gets to her.

Finally, it is time to go home. Paul had already gone for the day. I looked at Daniella and asked her if she is ready to go home and sleep on our next step and she agrees. Daniella states, "Maybe we should try a new approach tomorrow." I nod my head and agree. I'm beginning to get tired of the cat and mouse game. There must be a way to put an end to this.

Usually after I have had a good night's sleep, chocolate, and some coffee, I'm clear minded and can figure things out. Paul is bringing supper over tonight. My kind of guy. I do not like cooking, and it gets to be monotonous to eat TV dinners every night. Or my favorite, hot dogs. I know what you are thinking. Hot dogs are not the healthiest of foods, but they are good. And I can eat hot dogs fifty different ways. My favorite is a hot dog on a tortilla. Not sure why I like Mexican hot dogs. All I can say is don't knock it if you have not tried it. I'm not sure Paul would agree. He eats much healthier than I do. Surely after we have been married, I can sneak a hot dog or two.

Paul is at the door by 6:00 p.m. He has supper and chocolate. He is a keeper, that is for sure. How did he know I needed chocolate tonight? We prepare our plates and then we sit at the table with the wipe board in front of us. We are trying to figure out what the victims all have in common. What we have so far.

Victims profile:
Weak
Elderly with either money or a lot of prescriptions
Did not have a lot of family or friends
Gender does not seem to be a factor currently

We both agree this sounds like Michael. We need to continue to follow him, and we need to get him out of there.

We continue to eat and talk. Then we decide that we should have the chocolate next and race each other to the kitchen to get some. Turns out Paul likes chocolate as much as I do. I ask Paul if he will go to church with me. He has such a way with people. I told him about going to church and finding my grandmother, whom I did not know at the time she was my grandmother. Now I find out she is dead due to being overwhelmed at the sight of me. Nice! That is a first.

Paul says he would love to go to church with me. "Maybe some of these old ladies will talk to you and tell you what happened to my birth mother. If I could find her, I would like to invite her to our wedding." He agrees that would be a great idea.

And now that we know each other's background, we can relax a little bit. I will relax after I have some of my FBI friends check him out. What is that saying, "In God, I trust. All others I monitor." That about sums it up. Once he passes the check, we can move on, and he will never know that I checked, right?

Friday Again

Time flies when you are having fun chasing criminals. This has been a hard case to crack open. I wonder who will die, who will leave, who will get arrested next. At least the days are not dull. I would like to find out who is the mastermind behind the bullying gang soon so I can get on with that vacation I promised myself.

It is time to watch the cameras so we can see what Michael was up to last night. Surely, we can catch him doing something. We see him leaving work at 5:00 p.m. Then we see him go into several apartments of elderly women. As we watch the tape, we see several drug deals that take place. If only drug deals are my only concern. For now I need to concentrate on the murders that take place in this apartment complex. I would think that we have eliminated most of the gang members by now. Sometimes the evil gets blurred as it comes and goes in many different forms.

Daniella is very good at watching the cameras and finding things that I don't see since my attention span is usually shorter than a gold-fish. I guess I should ease up on the coffee and chocolate. As she goes through each camera from last night, she notices some activity in the maintenance shop. She watches Michael and notices he is hiding something back there. We go to the shop and begin our search.

He is very good at hiding things in plain sight. We can't find anything out of place. We decide to play around with his mind a little. We move some things out of place then go back to the cameras to see if that shakes him up at all.

We go back to the office as the phone is ringing and ringing. Seriously! Who wants to talk to us so badly they keep calling? The phone rings again, and I answer it. It is Tim Peterson, my boss and, I thought, friend. He does not sound very happy. Just saying! He wants to know how the investigation is going and what is taking so long. Really? You would think I could just come in here and find out about this gang, dismantle it, and go home. I try to explain to him that the gangs at the border are evil and they are also businessmen. That means they live by a totally different set of rules.

This gang, on the other hand, are not businesspeople, and even though they are in it for the money and for the drugs, they are crazy. This puts an entire new spin on the evil and takes so much more time and investigation. If you aren't careful, you will end up in their grave in the back yard somewhere. At least with the gang at the border, you know the enemy. Not so much here! Your informant could turn on you or die in the next minute. After explaining this to little Timmy (what I call him), he still does not get it. I ask him, "When was the last time he dealt with crazy people?" Okay, I will take that non-answer to mean he has not.

Being a little snarky, I suggest he comes and helps me so that we can end this soon. He does not see the humor in that suggestion. He also told me his boss wants this to wrap up soon. I told him I will do my best to get it done.

Chocolate Is Calling

Now I'm not only upset but I'm also being pressured. You know what that means. It is time to pull out all the stops.

1. Need chocolate
2. Need new clothes.
3. Need to have Paul investigated so that we can move on.
4. Need to talk to Daniella. There is nobody on the planet that is better at investigating.

We do not have Paul's Social Security number, but we have an address and a birthday. We also know that at one time he worked and lived in Pennsylvania. I talk to Daniella, and she states she is on it.

Now I must set up a sting to get Michael out of here. I can work on that until Daniella is done.

The Sting

The sting does not mean a bee. I need to set Michael up so I can catch him in the act. Once I get him out of the way then the next person, which I am assuming is the leader, will come out in the open. They will need to find somebody to replace Michael. Paul calls and wants to bring lunch for Daniella and me. We never turn down free food. Then we can finish our plans for the sting.

I am sitting with Daniella trying to discuss the sting and the last murder when suddenly we hear what we think was gunfire. We just look at each other and can't believe what is happening. Our training for an active shooter is ongoing. However, you never really believe it will happen to you. Once we have the blinds pulled and the lights out, we call 911. Once I was in active shooter training, we were told to time how long the police take to respond, and that is how long you must stay alive before help arrives. The last time we did this, it took forever for the police to respond. I know we are on our own, and it does not look pretty.

We crawled to the cameras so we could try to locate the shooter. Help is supposedly on the way. We can see him walking up and down the hallways waving his gun and yelling something. Who the heck is he looking for? We can't make out the name. Just about the time I think help is going to arrive, Paul shows up with our lunch. Oh no, not Paul. I try to call him, but I am not fast enough. He walks in the front door and is shot. By now my blood is boiling. Okay, maybe not really boiling, but I am upset. Now I call back to 911, tell them we have a person shot, not sure how many other people are going to need an ambulance.

The person on the other end of the phone states, "How bad is he shot?"

"I don't know," I reply.

Then she says, "Stay on the line with me."

I just laugh and put the phone down so she can listen to what happens next.

I look at Daniella, and she looks at me. Paul is lying in front of the office bleeding out. Where are the first responders, and where is that stupid shooter? I go to get my gun. Daniella just looks at me. "I did not know you were packing," she states. Some things are just better left unsaid.

Finally, I hear the first responders. I told Daniella to look at the cameras and see if there is any sighting of the shooter. I put my earpiece in and took my phone. I told her to keep me informed. I'm going out the back and see if I can see him, then I will work my way around to the front so that I can check on Paul.

Daniella agrees but is not happy at all about being left alone. By now I'm so mad I could just spit. Let me find that shooter and he will not shoot anybody else.

As I round the corner, I see Paul lying on the floor bleeding. I rush to him and hold him in my arms. "Paul, honey, please hold on. The first responders are here. Please don't die on me. I need you." The first responders come in and take charge of Paul. I ask them which hospital they are taking him to. Then I resume my search.

Now this has become personal. I do not know whom they are looking for, but I will find this guy, and well, you know, hand him over to the authorities. Unless he decides to shoot me first, then I will have to respond. I'm really starting to grow tired of this place and this job. Why can't I find this leader? Time to step up my game.

I am on my way to the hospital to see Paul. He is in critical condition, and they are not sure if he is going to make it. I ask to see him, and I sit with him for a while. I'm praying like I have never prayed before. He has got to wake up and live. As I sit there with Paul praying, I begin to think about this sting. Do we need to set the sting up for Michael or not? I'm thinking that if we just feed him some information then watch what he does, that would be the end of it. I will talk to Daniella in the morning. Things have got to look better after a good night's sleep.

As I get in my car to go home, I feel eyes on me. Who is watching me? Why are they watching me? Isn't it enough that Paul is fighting for his life and the office is a mess right now? I keep walking, but I pick up the pace. Once in my car, I lock the doors and head for home.

The Next Day

I FORGET THAT DANIELLA had an appointment and will not be in the office until after lunch on Wednesday. I can give her all the details when she returns. I open the window and go back to my desk. I will try to concentrate on my paperwork and look at the cameras this morning. As I am sitting there, I hear a noise in the back room. There it is again. That is no mouse. It sounds more like a rat. The doorbell rings, and I walk slowly to the window. As I try to make sense of what this person is saying to me, I hear my back door shut. I try to stay calm. After I address the issue in front of me, I decide to go to the cameras and see what is going on. I look on several cameras. I still do not see anybody.

What was that noise? Michael comes to the window to find out about the shooter. I explain to him that I do not have any more information than what we had yesterday. He looks a little defeated since I do not invite him in. I learned my lesson the hard way. I do not invite Michael in an office that I am alone in. I'm not afraid of him, but it would be a tough fight.

Michael walks away and appears to be going back to work. After I am satisfied that he is going to go back to working on whatever project he is working on, I continue my search. As I search, I realize I need to get that police dog soon so she can come to work with me.

I miss Daniella. It is very quiet here in the office with no other humans to talk to. As I settle back in my chair and try to get some of the dreaded paperwork done that has piled up over the day, I feel like somebody is watching me. There it is again, that feeling! I must be in some extreme need of chocolate and sleep. I keep working. I hate to admit it, but some of the sounds that this old building makes is scary, but we are used to it, and I don't really pay much attention to them anymore. Is somebody actually watching me, or am I just a little on edge after the shooting?

It is finally lunchtime. Daniella calls to let me know she won't be in the office until the afternoon as she has a family emergency. I told her that is okay, that I am leaving for lunch to visit Paul, and I will be back in the office around 2:00 p.m. I also remind her to let me know how her family is doing. She says she will.

Lunch is going to be hospital food while I sit with Paul. The hospital food is really good so that will not be a sacrifice. I just need to see if Paul is awake. I get checked in, which takes about twenty minutes, then I'm off to the cafeteria. I think today I will have their chicken. Love the chicken served at the hospital. I need a soda. Soda is not a good thing, but every now and again I need a soda. Today is an extra-large soda. It is going to be a long day. I just have that feeling. Once I am done here, I need to go back to work to make sure Michael hasn't stolen all my tools in the maintenance shop. Why do I keep him around when he is such a downer? I guess I would rather see him in jail than applying for unemployment. He won't get it even if he tried, but it takes more paperwork. I have told you I hate paperwork. Why do I have a job that has so much paperwork? And if the government ever tells you they are saving trees, just laugh because I feel like I go through a ream or two of paper every day.

Once I have my food, I head up to Paul's room. If he is awake, we can talk. Heck, even if he is not awake, we will talk. I can talk. He can listen to me. Maybe we can mind meld and he can give me some advice on how to handle this situation.

I tiptoe into his room. It is so dark in this little room. Doesn't anybody ever check on him? I open the curtains and turn on a small light. He is still sleeping. I pull up a chair and a table so I can eat and tell him everything that is happening in my world while he sleeps and is healing. I want to cry because I let this happen to him. Why did I not call him right away and tell him to stay off the property? Will I ever think? My job is so dangerous sometimes that I just take that for granted. Everybody around me should know this. Paul is not a stranger to danger, but he could never have seen that active shooter in the middle of the day happening.

I finish eating and telling him about my day. I kiss him and tell him I will be back tomorrow for lunch. He will always be my lunch buddy, and he needs to get better so we can eat at the cafeteria together. Then he can take me out for supper or we can eat supper at my house. I told him I'm getting a police dog in the very near future. "I will bring him by to see you as soon as I get him or her." The dog will be a working police dog, which means I can bring him to the hospital.

"It is 1:30 p.m., and I must leave now, Paul. I must go back to work. See you for lunch."

I go to my car, and there it is again. I feel somebody watching me. Maybe I'm just going insane, or I just have left over jitters from that active shooter. I have my gun, but what good is a gun if you can't see anything? When I get back to work, I am going to call the Oklahoma City Police. It is my understanding that they have a K-9 unit. They may be able to help me find a dog.

As I approach my office, it looks like some of the residents are waiting for me. Now isn't that just awesome? I will have to draw on some of my awesome customer service skills. Once I have the office open and I talk to each one, I go back to my desk and try to work on some of that pesty paperwork.

Next, I hear the bell chime, and there is Michael. Now what could he want at this late hour? I'm sure it is something ridiculous. I walk to the window, and Michael looks a little upset. It is almost 4:00 p.m. Do I really need to deal with this now? "Yes?" I say to Michael.

Michael asks me to come with him to the maintenance shop. There seems to be a problem, and he has to show me the problem rather than just tell me about it. I say, "Okay, but let me get a sign for the window." I also want to let Daniella know where I'm going in case I don't come back. So now I'm overdramatic. You never know! At least if I'm missing, they will look for me.

I close the window and put a sign in the window. Michael heads toward the shop. Why do I feel like this is wrong and that I'm a lamb being led to slaughter? There I go again being dramatic. I should have been a writer with the imagination that I have. Once in the shop, Michael closes the door, and I'm starting to feel, well, you know scared! He looks at me, and for one slight minute I think I see his eyes glow green, then he morphs into Michael.

By now I'm getting very impatient and ask what the emergency was. He looks at me and smiles. No emergency! I go to leave, and he grabs my hand. I look at him like he is crazy, and the laugh that comes out of his mouth is enough to make anybody cringe. Now I'm scared and mad all at the same time. However, my feelings are not of Michael's concern. He starts dragging me back to the back of the shop. I notice a door that was not there before. What is he up to? He opens the door and pushes me into the small room.

The small room is created to be soundproof, with a toilet, an opening for air, and down at the bottom of this small room is a place to slide a tray into. Okay, this is just a little creepy. How did I not see this coming? Surely Daniella will look for me when she comes back to work. Michael does not say much. He snickers and walks away. Why do they always snicker? What does that mean? Is he keeping me as his pet, or is he just waiting for Daniella to come so he can kill her too? I don't want to die. I don't want to be here, and I want to see Paul.

I sit down and begin to pray. I realize I will not be able to win this battle without some divine intervention. Nothing like a kidnapping to get you closer to God. As I pray, I fall asleep. I wake and believe it to be the next day as I have food and water in my little space. I eat my food. Guess Michael doesn't care if I have chocolate or not. Okay, the chocolate would have been a treat. If I'm going to die, at least give me chocolate. What does Michael want from me? I don't see an end game, unless he just wants to kill Daniella and I at the same time.

I pray Daniella is okay and that she can figure out where I'm at. I wish I have my phone and some communication with the outside world. I listen and I hear voices, no I'm not going crazy. I really hear voices. Sounds like Michael is talking to a contractor. Does the contractor not think it strange that the manager is not around? People, including myself, are sometimes clueless.

Next, I hear Michael gathering tools. Are you kidding me? He is going to go to work like nothing is wrong. When I get out of this place, he is in for a rude awakening, that is for sure. By now I'm starting to cry. I hate small spaces. I need chocolate and clean clothes.

My hair is a mess, and I am beginning to hate this guy, evil spirit, or whatever he is. You can be sure I'm not trusting anybody ever again.

Daniella arrives at work after lunch. She is looking everywhere for me. How strange her car is here and there is a note dated yesterday stating she is going to the shop with Michael. Now where could she be? Daniella looks at the cameras and sees me going into the shop with Michael, but I never come out of the shop. *Okay, that is just a little strange*, Daniella thinks to herself.

Daniella thinks and prays. Then she sends Michael on a run for supplies. He asks if anybody has seen Victoria today. Daniella states, "As a matter fact, I didn't really think much of it. I thought she was just out on property someplace. Why? Did you happen to talk with her?" Daniella asks Michael.

He looks stunned. "No, I have not seen her," Michael says.

Daniella gives him his list and sends him out the door with another maintenance person, and they go to get supplies. Once they are out the door and Daniella is positive they are gone, she goes to the shop and starts her search. She quietly moves through the rooms calling for Victoria. She reaches the back room and calls for Victoria. I start hitting the door and calling back. Daniella is trying to find a way to open the door. Once she does, I come flying out and breathing, taking deep breaths. "I hate small spaces," I tell Daniella. "Now let's get this door back the way it was and call the police."

Once the police get to the property, we all talk and decide the best way to handle this is to have two armed police officers hiding out in the lobby and one on the front porch. When Michael brings the receipt to the window, I will answer the window to see the look of shock on his face. Then we will arrest him. I'm sure once he is in a jail cell, he will sing like a bird.

We all agree, and we get ready to take our positions. We wait for Michael to appear and bring the receipt to the window. The doorbell rings, and I walk to the window. Look on his face, priceless! He snickers, then he turns to run. They run after him and apprehend him. I wave to him as he rolls away in a police car. Then we call in the other maintenance person to ask him what he knows about the crimes on this property. He is more than willing to give us the infor-

L.A. Ward

mation we need to take down the rest of the gang members on this property. He is quite hesitant to release the name of the leader as he is so scared she would have him killed. We assure him that we can protect him.

Finally, I get to go home to chocolate, a long hot shower, and some good food. Tomorrow we will get the little room taken down and work on the rest of the gang members. First, I need a good night's rest. Then I need to see Paul and call the K-9 unit in OKC for a police dog for protection. I am so exhausted.

170

The Day After

I AM GOING TO visit Paul in the hospital, and I tell Daniella I will stay with him until after lunch. There is no change. I keep praying. I have lunch with Paul, then I kiss him and tell him I will be back tomorrow at lunchtime to have lunch with him. I know what you are thinking, I am using this time with Paul to eat at the cafeteria because they have such good food. Shame on you! I would go and have lunch with Paul even if I have to bring lunch with me. But I sure do like that food in the cafeteria.

It is time to go back to work and wrap this up.

The other maintenance person gives us the name of the ring-leader. We just look at each other, and we call the police. When the police show up, we head up to A227. When we knock on the door, Betty Sue is not surprised. She just contours her little face and asks, "What took you so long?" She tries to stab the officer with her cane. I just can't believe my eyes. This cute little old lady who walks around with a cane, has bows in her hair, and always comes by the office to check on us is the leader. Turns out she is not all that old, just tiny. She wears a mask when she goes out, and her cane was a prop and a weapon.

Once she was in handcuffs, I just look at her and ask, "Why?" She just snickers. Of course she does.

Last Day at the Office

We finally have the entire gang either in jail or they have moved and will not be coming back. Michael is telling the police everything. How Betty Sue was in charge and how she controlled everything that was happening on the property. I am shocked. She looked like such a sweet little old lady.

Michael told the police how it was Betty Sue's idea to kidnap me and then she was going to kidnap Daniella. She was then going to sell us to the highest bidder. Really? Does this human trafficking stuff ever go away? Betty Sue can no longer hurt any of us. From what I understand, she just sits in her cell and snickers. Of course she does! When they get caught, it is always the snickering that gives them away. After this is quiet for a while, I need to visit her to find out why. Why she wanted to hurt all those people and why she hated us so badly.

The other residents are finally safe, and as one last act, I wrote a complete policy on bullying.

Policy: Bullying

> Bullying will not be tolerated at this apartment complex. Should you feel that you are a target of bullying, you must tell somebody. You must write an information form and hand it into the office, or you can put it in the drop box. If you are scared for your life, then give us times and dates we can see on camera what is going on. It is important that you talk to somebody, and you may want to report the problem to the police. Do not sit back and think at is okay to be the victim of bullying. Remember, bullying

happens in many different ways. They can target you on your cell phone, leave messages on your door, or they can say snarky remarks to you when they go past you. This is not normal and will disrupt your peaceful enjoyment while living at this apartment complex. Do not let this continue. See it, tell somebody.

The End

https://www.stopbullying.gov/

Are there federal laws that apply to bullying?

At present, no federal law directly addresses bullying. In some cases, bullying overlaps with discriminatory harassment, which is covered under federal civil rights laws enforced by the US Department of Education (ED) and the US Department of Justice (DOJ). No matter what label is used (e.g., bullying, hazing, teasing), schools are obligated by these laws to address the conduct when it meets all three criteria below. It is the following:

- Unwelcome and objectively offensive, such as derogatory language, intimidation, threats, physical contact, or physical violence;
- Creates a hostile environment at school. That is, it is sufficiently serious that it interferes with or limits a student's ability to participate in or benefit from the services, activities, or opportunities offered by a school; and is
- Based on a student's race, color, national origin, sex, disability, or religion
  o Sex includes sexual orientation, gender identity, and intersex traits. Sex also includes sex-based stereotypes and sexual harassment.
  o National origin harassment can include harassment because a student speaks another language.
  o DOJ also has jurisdiction to enforce Title IV of the Civil Rights Act of 1964, which addresses certain equal protection violations based on religion in public schools. Title VI of the Civil Rights Act of 1964, enforced by both ED and DOJ, does not explicitly identify religion as a basis for prohibited discrimination. But religious-based harassment is often based on shared ancestry of ethnic characteristics, which is covered under Title VI.

While these laws apply to students being bullied, in the great state of Oklahoma, you can still use these guidelines if you are elderly and being bullied. Do not let anybody steal your peaceful enjoyment in life are they may try to steal your life next. Always speak up and tell somebody.

Printed in the USA
CPSIA information can be obtained
at www.ICGtesting.com
LVHW050404210624
783560LV00002B/389

9 798889 828679